D1187748

Haunted Pass

James Deadwood is a legend, a man with a reputation for always bringing his quarry to justice – usually in a pine box. But within hours of riding into the hell town of Autumn Pass, an ambush leaves him a bullet-ridden corpse.

Sent to investigate the death of the 'fastest gun in the West', ex-manhunter Jim Hannigan and his partner Angela del Pelado soon discover all is not as it appears. And after Deadwood's ghost shows up, the two are led on a trail of murder and deceit. Soon they are in danger of disappearing too.

Haunted Pass

Lance Howard

A Black Horse Western

ROBERT HALE · LONDON

© Howard Hopkins 2007
First published in Great Britain 2007

ISBN 978-0-7090-8270-5

Robert Hale Limited
Clerkenwell House
Clerkenwell Green
London EC1R 0HT

www.halebooks.com

The right of Howard Hopkins to be identified as
author of this work has been asserted by him
in accordance with the Copyright, Designs and
Patents Act 1988

Typeset by
Derek Doyle & Associates, Shaw Heath
Printed and bound in Great Britain by
Antony Rowe Limited, Wiltshire

For Tannenbaum

Please visit Lance Howard on the web at:
www.howardhopkins.com

CHAPTER ONE

Here was a place old gunfighters came to die. . . .

James Deadwood couldn't have told why that thought invaded his mind as he pushed through the batwings of the Wild Bull saloon, but it did. A niggling, bedeviling thing, he couldn't force it away.

A cloud of Durham smoke assailed his nostrils as he stopped just inside the doors and surveyed the barroom. The scent was pleasant but it came fouled with the odors of old vomit, stale booze and the copiously applied cheap perfume that reeked from the handful of whores working the Sodom-like establishment.

A deuce of steps took him to the edge of the short landing, where he paused, squinting, gaze roving, then descended the three steps to the saloon proper. The place might have been Hell's mirror, he reckoned. He'd visited countless dens of drink and iniquity, blacked out in only a handful fewer, but Autumn Pass's saloon rivaled the best – or worst – of them. Always had.

How many years had it been since he'd set foot

within its lust- and vice-filled walls? Twenty, perhaps? The place had not changed a lick. The faces of the whores were different, but the rule remained the same: grab everything from the moment, and to hell with tomorrow's consequences.

His kind of place, that was for damn sure.

A large room, it was jammed with cowboys from the town's neighboring ranches, men lured by the siren calls of games of chance and gals of the line. Gamblers – pros and tinhorns alike – tested their luck. Myriad unsavory types, men who roved the owlhoot, the very men James Deadwood professed to chase down, bring to justice or eliminate completely, occupied gloomy corners.

A rowdy chorus of laughter from soiled women, whoops of joy from game-winners and curses from losers punctuated the enharmonic clanking of a tinkler piano. He took a notion to shoot the player, a scarecrow of a fellow wearing a black armband, but better judgement persuaded him that wasn't the entrance he wanted to make. He had more important business in this town; why jeopardize it over something as paltry as raw nerves?

Sighing, he searched for any sign of the man he expected might be awaiting him, but glimpsed no sign of the sonofabitch.

'Dammit, Edgecomb,' he whispered.

He spotted a bargirl giving him a lust-painted expression as her slim hand drifted over the breast of her purple-sateen bodice. A pretty little thing with ringlets of red hair, she had the plump lips and freckle-kissed face to which he was partial. He'd give her a tumble later, after he determined whether Edgecomb would show up tonight, and after he'd indulged in the other luxuries the Wild Bull had to offer.

His attention shifting from the dove, he worked his way to the polished bar that ran nearly the entire length of the north wall. Behind the bar a 'keep who'd seen too many steak dinners stood wiping out a glass while absently gazing into the gilt-edged, cracked mirror that hung between two hutches stocked with bottles.

The barman eyed him with a raised eyebrow, recognition jumping into his small eyes.

James Deadwood reckoned he hadn't changed all that much in twenty years. His face might have become a bit more gaunt, his six-foot-four frame a hair more wiry, but the dark eyes that peered from a pale skull were still the same. Dark brown, nearly black, they were the eyes of a soul trapped in an abyss, a soul he had long ago relinquished to the demons with which he grappled.

He still wore his signature frock-coat and twin Colts stuck in a red-silk sash at his waist. Brown-blond hair that just touched his angular shoulders straggled from beneath a battered felt hat. A soup-strainer mustache dangled to his chin. Legends did best not to alter their appearance, he reckoned, unless they wanted to be legends no more – or wanted to vanish.

Had anyone asked, James Deadwood would have told them he was a man who embraced his reputation, or more accurately, his infamy, as many scribes chose to call it. Frankly, he didn't give a damn what label they applied to him as long as they never forgot he was the fastest gun who had ever lived.

'Gawddamn, if I ain't died and gone straight to hell!' the barkeep said, setting the glass on the bartop, then slapping a palm against the wood.

Deadwood offered a wispy smile, pleased that the man recognized him. 'Hell's a right proper name for this hole. How's business, Bartholomew?'

The 'keep nodded, a motion that reminded Deadwood of a distressed bantam cock. 'Women have bottoms and the bottles don't, as the sayin' goes. Figured you for dead. You come back to haunt this place?'

Deadwood leaned against the bar, fingers absently playing with the gold watch-chain dangling from his vest pocket. His gaze never settled, however, and at any instant he knew fully what was going on about him. Too many owlhoots and young guns hoped to carve a rep by killing a legend; he wasn't ready to cash in his chips just yet.

'Legends never die, Bart, don't you know that?' He winked, ran his tongue over his top teeth. 'How 'bout a bottle of something that ain't like to turn me into a spook?'

The barman chuckled and reached behind him, yanking a bottle of Orchard from the hutch. Deadwood fished in a pocket for a double eagle, but the 'keep waved a hand. 'Your money's no good here, Mr Gunfighter. Ain't often we get a celebrity in this place. Just don't go killin' none of my regulars.'

Deadwood glanced behind him at the selection of hardcases populating the barroom. 'I'll try to restrain myself. Tonight's a night for cards and women – aces and asses, I like to say. Plenty of time for death later.'

'Can't say that's the first time I heard that promise out of you, but it might be the first time you held to it, iffen you leave here tonight without a body tally.'

Deadwood laughed, the sound as abrasive as a demon chuckling. 'You always did fret too much, Bart. But thank you kindly for the whiskey.'

Deadwood grabbed the bottle and swung from the bar, glancing again at the room. Momentarily his line of sight drifted to the mezzanine balcony that ran along the south wall, above the stairway leading to the upper rooms where the whores plied their trade. He smiled, imagining what he would do to that little red-headed filly later. He never had been able to control his rough lovemaking after a bottle of Orchard.

His gaze lowered and he noticed a couple men eyeing him, both outlaws. Their eyes averted the moment he tipped a finger to his hat. His reputation was alive and kickin', he reckoned, and if either of those men planned to live out the night they'd leave him be.

With a sigh, he threaded his way towards a rear table. An empty seat at a poker-game with a decent pot of cash, coin and personal items such as gold watches and silver cufflinks provided an irresistible invitation for a man addicted to the vices offered in

11

an establishment as riotous as the Wild Bull. Hell, Edgecomb was nowhere to be seen, anyway.

As he reached the table he eyed the man sitting with his back to the wall. The cowboy gazed up from his cards, sweat beaded on his brow, crimson rouging his cheeks. Losing powerful bad, Deadwood wagered, and eager for some new blood, preferably greenhorn blood.

'Mind if I sit in, fellas?' Deadwood held up his Orchard bottle. 'Got me a stake and a bottle I'm willin' to share.'

The cowboy nodded, and the three others at the table voiced grunts of approval.

'Take a seat, gent,' the cowboy said, with a flick of his hand indicating the empty chair.

Deadwood nodded his thanks. 'Mind if I take yours, gent?'

'My what?' The little cowboy's brow crinkled.

'Chair. Never play cards 'less I can sit with my back to the wall.'

The man eyed him with a puzzled expression, then shrugged and stood. 'Suit yourself.' He settled in the empty seat while Deadwood slid into the one the man had vacated.

'Thank you kindly, gent.' Deadwood opened the bottle and poured two fingers of whiskey into each man's glass. Finished, he swallowed a generous gulp from the bottle and leaned back against the wall. Liquid fire seared its way down his throat and settled like a camp-fire on a chilled night in his belly.

'You got a particular reason for thinking you

might get backshot?' the little cowboy asked, dealing a hand and casting Deadwood a sideways glance.

Deadwood swept up his cards, studied them, then looked back to the man. 'None I'd care to recite. Tonight's strictly aces and asses.'

The man's brow cinched. 'What?'

Deadwood smiled, a snakelike thing. 'Win or lose, I aim to have that little redhead yonder.' He ducked his chin towards the woman, who was gazing at him with smoky blue eyes that promised untold pleasures.

The little man's gaze went in that direction and he laughed. 'See your point, now. That's Tilda. Comes from the East somewhere. Heard tell she knows things women shouldn't know.'

Deadwood licked his lips. 'Then I reckon she'll be teachin' 'em to me 'fore the dawn.'

That was the extent of the conversation for the next few hours, except for the occasional request for another shot of Orchard and staccato outbursts that turned the air blue after Deadwood cleaned them out of their earnings and personal effects. The little cowboy folded first, the look on his features mirroring how much of an idiot he figured himself for because he'd allowed the stranger in the frock-coat into the game in the first place. Two hours later, the table had cleared but for one man, a burly fellow barely able to hold up his head.

'Lay 'em,' the man said, spittle bubbling at the corners of his lips.

Deadwood felt only a fraction more coherent

than his game-mate; the empty whiskey bottle before him testified to that fact. He dropped his cards onto the table, two aces and two eights, as black as his gaze. He felt certain he'd beaten whatever hand the other man held. He couldn't focus enough to read the cards but he reckoned the furious expression that washed across the other's face said it all.

'You goddamn cheater!' the man blurted, coming half out of his seat. Whiskey had eroded not only his playing ability but his common sense.

Deadwood's arms circled the pot and he swept it towards him. 'Count your losses, friend, and count yourself lucky I'm in a horny mood instead of a killin' one.'

'The hell I will! You won damn near every hand. Nobody plays that good. You musta been cheatin'.'

Deadwood's eyes half-cleared, narrowed, locking on the man. 'I never cheat at cards. You weren't so lubricated you might've played better, but it wasn't your night. Be thankful I don't take a notion to plug that leak in your mouth permanently.'

Even in his drunken condition the fella tensed. A second later his hand made the slightest motion towards the gun at his belt. It wasn't a committed move and Deadwood was glad of it, otherwise he would have had to break his promise to the 'keep. He still might have to, but the man had a marginal chance of walking out of the saloon under his own power instead of being carried out in a box.

It happened before the man could see it or Deadwood could think about it. With a blurring of his hand, his Colt whisked from the sash at his belt and leveled on the man's chest. Given his condition, it was not the smoothest draw he'd ever made, but it proved sufficient.

The man froze, hand in mid-motion, eyes wide as bowls. 'Maybe . . . maybe I was mistaken after all. . . .' he muttered, hand relaxing, dropping to his side.

'Reckon you owe me an apology.' Had words ever been spoken more coldly, Deadwood figured this man couldn't have testified to them.

Hesitation and anger flashed across the man's face with the request, but he had sobered enough for good sense to win out. 'I, uh, I'm sorry, gent. Sorry I called you a cheater. You won fair and square.'

Deadwood laughed, keeping his aim on the man. 'Get the hell out of here 'fore I take a notion not to be so kindly. Tomorrow you can tell whoever gives a damn you went up against the legendary James Deadwood and walked away with your life and without your balls.'

The man's face bleached, recognition of the name making him shudder. With a jackrabbit nod he backed away. Deadwood holstered his Colt as soon as the man had stumbled through the batwings out into the night.

The 'keep, who'd been eyeing Deadwood, frowned. Deadwood grinned, spreading his hands. Bart shook his head, disgust soiling his lips, then went back to pouring a glass.

James Deadwood gripped the edge of the table

and hoisted himself out of his chair. He spent a moment endeavoring not to topple over, then stuffed his winnings into whatever pocket would hold them. He pulled his gold watch from his vest and checked the time, but was unable to focus on the hands, so he returned the timepiece to the pocket.

Maneuvering around the table, he struggled to steady himself. An arm suddenly thrust beneath his and he looked over to see the red-haired dove grinning at him, helping him stay on his feet.

'You ready for Tilda, now, gent?' she asked, her free hand revealing a glimpse of her breast as she tugged at the bodice top.

His legs nearly buckled with the bolt of arousal that sizzled through him. He regained his composure and gave her a lustful grin. 'Reckon as ready as I'll ever be. I hear tell you got things to teach me. . . .'

She laughed, a lilting, yet hard-edged sound. 'I got mysteries in store for you you can't even imagine, James Deadwood.'

He peered at her. 'You know my name?'

Her grin widened. 'Don't everybody?'

He might have caught something amiss in her voice then, had he been sober, but any fleeting sense of caution dissolved with the sensation of her fingertips dragging across his chest.

He let her guide him to the stairs leading to the upper level, his steps graceful as a mule attempting a two-step.

Getting up the stairs was an exercise in stumbles

and near plunges that would have ended with a broken neck. Tilda anchored him, small but strong, but she had all she could do to support his six-foot-four frame.

By dumb luck and the grace of the Devil they reached the top, then stumbled along the mezzanine to a dimly lit hallway. Lanterns, flames turned low, flickered on the walls. Shadows and butter jittered over red-striped foil wallpaper.

'Number four's my room,' Tilda said, steering him down the hall.

A shiver trickled through him, a brief, ill-defined thing. Why? He couldn't have told, but his legs wobbled and his balls tingled. When her free hand drifted below the silk sash at his waist any caution disappeared with the thought of how the young woman's naked body would feel pressed against his.

At room four, Tilda propped him against the wall beside the door, then plucked a skeleton key from her bodice. She giggled and he smiled, trying not to drool. Damn, how was he ever going to get his pecker working, feeling this lubricated?

She swung the door inward, then stepped back, hand sweeping out in a gesture for him to enter. He glanced at the open room, which was dark, then pushed himself away from the wall and staggered inside.

A lantern came on and he froze, the shiver from a few moments before returning, stronger, sobering him a measure.

An instant later the bore of derringer pressed against the back of his neck.

17

'Sugar, for some hell-and-leather legend you sure were an easy mark.' A harsh giggle punctuated her words.

He remained still, other than to lift both his hands, and cursed himself for his sloppiness.

'I didn't expect to die so soon. . . .' he whispered.

Another laugh came from Tilda. 'Who ever does?'

The derringer came away from his neck and Tilda backed into the hallway, pulling the door closed behind her.

She stuffed the derringer back into her bodice.

An instant later, shots rang out from within the room.

One night later. . . .

Tilda Sorenson staggered along the mezzanine overlooking the barroom, the world spinning before her eyes. She stepped to the railing and peered down at the rowdy crowd, giggling, thinking of the windfall she'd come into last night, some of which she'd spent on a bottle of Bart's best gin. She'd taken the night off from whoring, deciding to experience life from the other side of the tracks at least once.

Boring, she decided. Smelly, drooling men playing games of chance, fondling whores and belching, some keeling over dead drunk, or tossing their belly contents after too many rounds of redeye. Their lives were no better than hers, and tomorrow she'd go back to making money on her back. Whoring was all she knew how to do anyhow and the windfall would vanish after a few nights with Dr. Laudanum and Nurse Gin.

She pushed herself away from the railing, falling back into the thick shadows that cavorted along the landing. With a sideways tilt, she made a *pfft* sound, gave a dismissing wave of her hand to the rowdies below and wandered into the hallway. She headed towards her room, where she planned to sleep off the gin till noon the next day.

The hallway looked darker than on the previous night, when she'd led that overrated gunfighter gent up here, but likely it was just the booze.

Tilda. . . .

'Huh?' she mumbled, not sure whether she'd really heard a whispering of her name or was merely too steeped to tell it from a voice in her head.

Come closer, Tilda . . . I need you tonight. . . .

She paused, the hallway jittering before her vision. She had heard a voice, a silky whisper. The sound hadn't come from her head. She peered into the buttery gloom cast from the low-turned wall lanterns.

She took a couple of stumbling steps, gaze wandering to door number four, the room to which she'd taken Deadwood. The door was ajar, darkly inviting.

'Is someone there?' Her voice shook more than she would have expected and a chill slithered down her spine. Wasn't like her to get all jiggered over some silly voice. Tilda Sorenson wasn't scart of a gawddamn thing!

Tilda . . . come to me. . . .

'Who are you?' she asked, voice jumping from her mouth as if chased out by some creature of the night. 'What the hell'shoo want?'

I want you, Tilda . . . I want your body next to mine . . . Come to me . . . I'll pay you generously. . . .

She paused, thinking it over. What the hell, all she had to do was lie on her back and a few extra bits couldn't hurt. She felt close to blacking out anyway. Good money for no real work.

'Where are you?' Her eyes narrowed.

Here, Tilda . . . in room four . . . waiting for you. . . .

'Room four?' She took staggering steps in that direction. Room four. She hoped they'd scrubbed the blood off the floorboards.

On reaching the door she leaned against the jamb and peered inside. The interior was pitch black and she couldn't see a thing. She pushed the door open wider and stepped into the room.

'Where are you? Why you got no lights on?'

Close the door, Tilda. I'll fire a lantern. . . .

'Hmmph,' she muttered, but flung the door shut behind her.

Come to me, Tilda . . . Closer. . . .

'You said you'd light the lant—'

Hands locked about her throat, choking off all sound. Fingers pressed deep into her soft flesh, crushing her windpipe with a brittle dead-leaf sound. Tears flooded her eyes, brought by welts of pain and overpowering terror.

You're a loose end, Tilda . . . can't allow that, now, can I?

The words were no more than a hiss against the

roar pounding in her ears. She struggled, desperately pried at the hands clamped to her throat and kicked at the shins of an attacker she couldn't see. Her mind washed sober the instant she knew with all certainly that Death had found her in this room. Deeper blackness swarmed through her mind and fragments of her sordid life flashed across her numbed brain. An instant later she swore she saw a demon waiting to greet her at the gates of Hell.

CHAPTER TWO

'You plan to let me in on the details of this mission, or just make it a big ol' surprise when we get there?' Tootie del Pelado, sitting atop a bay, cast a sideways look at Jim Hannigan, whose gaze remained fixed on the leaf-strewn trail ahead. She grinned and poked up her hat to let bright autumn sunlight wash across her face. The chilly air had rouged her cheeks, giving her face an angelic quality that made Jim Hannigan think he just might have been the luckiest man in the West to have her at his side.

He glanced at her, smiling a smile he knew would likely irritate the hell out of her, but unable to stop himself. Old habits died hard.

'Wipe it off your puss, Hannigan,' Tootie said, raising an eyebrow. 'I'm not some little woman along for the ride anymore. Not since that night in Angel Pass. . . .' She winked and a shiver traveled through him.

He shifted in the saddle, his rangy frame stiff from the ride, his hindquarters protesting against the roan's constant jarring as it navigated the uneven trail.

His gaze swept forward. Autumn Pass, their destination, lay only a mile or two ahead. His eyes narrowed as he tugged the reins to guide the big roan around a large rock jutting from the middle of the rutted trail. It had rained the previous night, the downpour followed by a bright moon and deep frost that the early-morning sunlight was only now beginning to melt. The musky aroma of decaying leaves and the perfume of blue spruce fragranced the air.

To either side of the trail a panorama of red, orange, and blazing yellow sparkled with sunlight. For one of the few times in his career he wished there was no mission, that he could simply spend time with the woman riding beside him, perhaps a picnic, a long walk, an afternoon of lovemaking.

Christ, you're going soft, Hannigan. That can't be a good sign. . . .

He chuckled, but stopped immediately when he noticed Tootie studying him.

'Don't see as how I said anything particularly funny.' The look she gave him made him turn even redder, because that look said she was reading his innermost thoughts. Trail-worn manhunters simply didn't indulge in flights of fancy and thoughts of romance and she thought it grandly amusing, he could tell. She enjoyed it and wanted more.

Well, at least her mood had brightened over the past few days. After leaving her brother behind in Angel Pass melancholy had gripped her, plunged her into the dark world of her thoughts. Things had happened in that town that would haunt her for the

23

rest of her life, no matter how strong she tried to appear. And Jim Hannigan was a man who knew a thing or two about being haunted.

'Wasn't laughing at what you said.' He hoped she'd let it go at that.

'Figured as much.' Her gaze shifted back to the trail. 'Care to enlighten me?'

'Not particularly.'

'Figured that, too. You seem a mite distracted. Anything to do with me?'

'Nope.' Damn, he'd said that too reflexively.

'I see.' The look on her face told him he hadn't pulled anything over on her. 'Reckon I once mighta said you were a poor liar. . . .'

'James Deadwood,' he said, wanting to get off the subject.

'Who?'

'James Deadwood. Figured you might have heard of him.'

'Reckon I'm not as world-wise as you.'

He eyed her. 'Was that sarcasm from Miss del Pelado?'

She laughed a gentle laugh. 'That was fact, Mr Jim Hannigan.'

He shrugged. 'James Deadwood, the fastest gun in the West, if you believe what's been written about him.'

'Any reason not to?'

'Reckon not, though I never was one to take the written word very serious, especially the kind set down in dime novels. But most legend is built on some kind of fact and it's a near certainty he's killed over fifty men.'

A small gasp escaped Tootie's lips. 'Fifty? What the devil is he?'

'A bounty man, of sorts. Can't recall him ever bringing a killer back alive, though, and more than one of his kills was based on circumstantial evidence and slippery logic.'

'You ever meet him?'

'Once. We worked a case together, but he was always going off on his own. Brought our quarry down before I got the chance to figure out whether the man was guilty or innocent. Deadwood never gives his targets a chance.'

'That's part and parcel of your job, isn't it?'

Hannigan sighed. 'I reckon. But Deadwood, he had an arrogance about him, a . . . I dunno, *darkness*, I guess you could call it. When you looked in his eyes you'd see plain nothin' sometimes. Other times . . . well, you ever seen a Blue Norther approaching?'

Tootie nodded. 'Few years back.'

'That's the look I saw in him. A dark storm coming, one he fought to hold off but couldn't. Rumor held him up as the West's greatest hero, but I heard whispers, ones that said he might just have been the West's worst killer.'

'You met him, what did you think?'

'Didn't care a lick for him and he returned the feeling. Got the notion he considered me competition instead of help. After the case ended we went our separate ways. Ain't seen him since. That was maybe eight years back. He rode with a partner sometimes, man by the name of Edgecomb. I never met the fella and didn't have enough time to locate his whereabouts before we set out.'

'We're going after Deadwood now, I take it? He did something that crossed the line?'

Hannigan shifted, rolling his shoulders. 'He was murdered last week, in a town called Autumn Pass. Got a note from my Pinkerton friend asking me to look into the case.'

'Why don't the Pinkertons do it themselves?' Tootie flicked a bug off her blouse, then smoothed her riding-skirt.

'Case is closed officially. The man's dead and the law accepts that.'

'But your friend doesn't?'

Hannigan shook his head. 'He's got a notion somethin' else is going on. Autumn Pass has a reputation for harboring owlhoots, so that Deadwood got his ticket punched there comes as no surprise. But from what my friend says they were bringing down charges against him that would have put a noose around his neck. Multiple murders of innocent men who Deadwood claimed were outlaws. My friend thinks Deadwood was in with the real outlaws and purposely killed others so the real hardcases could escape.'

'But if he's dead. . . .'

'*If.* Our mission is to take a look at his body and confirm he's boots up. Should be simple.'

She laughed. 'I've heard that before. . . .'

'Losing prospect whichever way it goes, I figure.'

'How so?'

'If he's dead, a cold-blooded killer goes out a legend. History books will paint him as a hero, way they do some other men of the West who are little more than sadistic butchers. If he's alive . . . well, he's a dangerous man and he or I ain't likely to just walk away from a confrontation under our own power.'

A note of worry crossed Tootie's face. 'I could do this alone, Jim. I could get in and take a look at the body. And if he is still alive he'd never suspect a woman coming after him.'

He glanced at her, frowning. 'You don't really think I'd let that happen, do you?'

She cast him a look. 'You don't really think I'd give you a choice? We're partners, in case you forgot.'

An easy laugh came from his lips. 'How could I? You never miss your chance to remind me.'

'Wouldn't be doing my job if I did.' She smiled. 'You got a picture of this Deadwood?'

He reined up. Tootie followed suit, angling her horse beside his. He rummaged through his saddle-bags and brought out a tintype. He passed it to her and her gaze locked on the shot of a man with dark barren eyes and a chimney-sweeper mustache who stood holding a Winchester by the barrel, the stock against the floor, his leg propped on a stool.

Tootie's face bleached. Her hands began to quiver and her lips parted slightly.

'What's wrong?' Hannigan asked.

She shook her head slowly, hands tightening on the tintype. The breeze stirred the wisps of blue-black hair that straggled from beneath her hat. She remained silent for dragging moments.

'Tootie?' he prodded. The silence had become eerie, strained. A gust kicked up dead leaves, sending them tumbling across the trail. His horse snorted.

Tootie shivered, licked her lips. 'I . . . I don't know . . . this man. . . .'

'That's Deadwood, a publicity photograph he did for some dime novel he was endorsing 'bout a year back. Most recent one I could find of him.'

'There's something about him. I don't know what it is but I've seen him somewhere before . . . and wherever it was, whatever it was in reference to . . . one thing I know for sure: this man is no legend.'

He pried the tintype from her death-grip on it, then stuffed it back into the saddlebag. 'I'm inclined to agree. You don't recollect where you saw him?'

She shook her head. 'No . . . no, I. . . .' She shuddered and he wondered just how Deadwood could have affected her so deeply that she couldn't bring the memory of their meeting to mind.

'We don't have to do this, Tootie. I took this case as a favor. I could have a marshal friend do it for me.'

'No!' Her voice came sharp. 'We have to do it now. I have to. That man's face . . . I won't be able to get it out of my mind if I don't make sure he's dead. Don't ask me why but I need to see his body, Jim. I need to know he's gone.'

He nodded, wondering just what it was about

Deadwood that had rattled her so, but he would give her time to figure it out.

'We're close to Autumn Pass. We best get this done, then.'

She nodded, then clucked her tongue and sent her horse into a brisk walk. He followed suit.

The day warmed but still carried a chill by the time they reached Autumn Pass. The town was ablaze in fall sunlight and a handful of folks scuttled along the boardwalks. The wide main street opened into various alleys and held convoluted twists, its layout seemingly designed by a drunken architect with little eye for design or grace. It seemed tranquil enough at the moment, but its reputation for bawdiness and bodies was well-known.

Why had Deadwood come here?

Hannigan had spent a day researching the bounty man's recent activities, collecting various newspaper accounts of his passings and had learned little more than that wherever Deadwood went bodies followed. His death-count had slowed of late and two articles quoted him as saying he was looking to retire. A couple other pieces covered the fact that certain men wished to bring him to justice, see to it that he was exposed for the killer they thought him to be. The notion had started as a spark and roared into a blaze, with some of the Territory's most powerful politicians backing the measure to invite him to a hanging – his own. Had Deadwood seen the direction the wind was blowing? Most certainly. He was arrogant but cagey, to Hannigan's recollection.

Had he come to Autumn Pass seeking help of some kind, searching out someone shady from his past who might help him avoid a necktie party? Possibly. Perhaps that plight had resulted in his death. The man might have been an outlaw in his own right but his reputation was wide and many owlhoots would be gunning for him, especially in a den of iniquity such as Autumn Pass.

As he came from his thoughts, Hannigan peered at the wide rutted street, scanning the rows of shops, false-fronted buildings and saloon. His focus settled on the marshal's office a block down, and he headed in that direction, Tootie in step beside him.

When he reached the office he reined up, spotting a heavyset man sitting on a chair on the boardwalk. The man was wearing a heavy hide coat and a young woman with auburn hair. Dressed in a peek-a-boo blouse and worn skirt, she had her hands pressed against his chest and was straddling him in the chair. His beefy hand was clamped to her left bosom. As she leaned in and kissed him, Hannigan cast Tootie a glance, then looked back to the lawdog.

'Fun starts early in these parts,' Tootie muttered, with a look of disgust.

'I ain't a prude,' Hannigan said in a loud voice, 'but I reckon fondling a whore in public is still frowned upon in most towns.'

The woman pulled back from the man and Hannigan could see his badge now. The marshal eyed him, then frowned. He was round-faced, with a beard and mustache that grew unbridled. Stains peppered his shirt. The woman, more a girl, despite a heavy coating of war paint she used to make herself look older, avoided looking at him and Tootie. The marshal shoved her off. She landed on her rear on the boardwalk with a distressed and oddly sad expression.

'Hey, you smelly sonofa—' she started.

'Get the hell out of here, Annalea.' The marshal's tone brooked no argument.

The girl rose to her feet, the sad look strengthening. 'I best still be getting paid.'

'You'll get what you got comin', don't worry about that.' The marshal smiled, which obviously irritated the girl, but she spun on a boot-toe and ran off.

'You're the marshal?' Hannigan said, making the sarcasm in his voice plain. He sized up the man without much trouble. Lazy, stupid and on the take. Little more to him than that.

'That's what this here badge says, fella.' The marshal fingered the star pinned to his breast, apparently missing Hannigan's tone. 'And your timing couldn't be worse. She's the prettiest whore we got.'

'Looks like the youngest, too, you dirty buzzard,' Tootie said, challenge in her voice. Jim could tell she had tallied the marshal's attributes and found them lacking.

The lawman's gaze softened as it raked Tootie's form in the saddle. An appreciative look came into his eyes. 'Well, I'd likely pay double for a fine filly such as your ownself.'

31

'You couldn't afford me,' she said, her expression smug mixed with disgust. 'And if you could I'd be too much for your fat ugly hide to handle.'

The marshal glared at her, as if uncertain whether to be insulted or aroused.

'Name's Jim Hannigan. I'm here about James Deadwood.' Jim shifted in the saddle, gaze drilling the marshal, whose look switched to something unreadable as he focused on the manhunter.

'Hannigan?' the marshal said, a mumble. He tugged his coat closed, as if suddenly chilled.

'You've heard of me, I take it?' Hannigan's gaze held the lawdog's.

'There a lawman who ain't?' The marshal's voice came stronger now, almost defiant.

'Then you know it'd be best to work with me instead of against.'

'That so?' The man's gaze jumped from Hannigan to Tootie, then back again.

Tootie's face cinched as the lawdog pushed his hat off his forehead. 'I know you from somewhere?' she asked.

The marshal heaved himself out of the chair, belly seeming to unroll as he did so. 'Think I'd recollect iffen I met a woman like you before. Reckon you'd never forget me, neither.' The marshal grabbed himself in a lewd gesture.

Tootie's eyes narrowed with disgust. 'Do that again and you'll be chasing 'em down the board-walk.'

The marshal laughed. 'I love me a feisty gal, I do.'

Hannigan suppressed the urge to pummel the

man. The more the marshal talked and the more he eyed Tootie the less Hannigan liked him.

'Tell me about Deadwood,' Hannigan said, voice firm.

The marshal scratched his armpit, then shrugged. 'What's to tell? The man got his ticket punched.'

'How?' Hannigan leaned forward in the saddle, rested a forearm across the horn.

'At the saloon. Was playing cards, got himself a little lubricated and let a whore lead him to his doom.'

'How'd he die?'

The marshal's small eyes glittered. The questioning clearly annoyed him but at the same time he appeared reluctant to push a man like Jim Hannigan too far.

'Like I said, he was drunk. We get a lot of hard-cases in this town, especially at the saloon, and a man like Deadwood attracts fellas lookin' to make a name for theirselves by killin' a legend.'

'You catch the men who did it?' Hannigan watched the lawdog closely, studying his features for any twitch of an expression that indicated a lie.

'No, they escaped.'

'They shoot him? Use a knife?'

The marshal frowned. 'The girl lured him up to a room above the saloon and he was bushwhacked. Shot to death.'

'What about this whore, she escape, too?'

The marshal shifted feet, looking suddenly uneasy. 'Not exactly.'

'Not exactly?' Tootie asked. 'What does that mean?'

'She got her ownself killed the next day. Some fella strangled her. Likely she deserved it.'

'How you figure?' Hannigan asked.

'Well, she led Deadwood to his death, so only fair fate'd get even.'

'Why didn't you arrest her before that happened?'

'Why should I? Ain't likely she knew what she was doin' or about those men waiting on him.'

Hannigan's eyes narrowed. 'Thought you just said she deserved it for leading him to his doom. . . .'

'Well, uh, yeah, she did, but that don't mean she knew what she was doing. She made a mistake.'

Hannigan uttered a sarcastic chuckle. 'And you ain't big on second chances.'

The marshal shrugged. 'Who cares? She was just a whore.'

Hannigan heard Tootie let out a *pfft* of disgust. 'When I said men you answered without hesitation; how do you know it was more than one?'

The marshal remained silent a moment, face tightening, eyes shifting. 'Uh, well, someone saw two men rushing out of the saloon in the commotion that followed. Heard more than one gunshot, too, so I figure there was at least two of them.'

Hannigan got the notion the man was lying. 'You look for them at all, try to track them?'

'Did my best.'

The man was lying through his teeth, but Hannigan let it go for the time being.

'Who identified the body, determined cause of death?'

The marshal scratched his armpit again. 'Well, I did, and Doc Butler.'

Hannigan straightened. 'Doc Butler's office is where?'

The marshal ducked his chin south. 'Down two blocks, on the right. He ain't usually in 'til sometime past noon. Don't like being disturbed before that, you get my meanin'.'

'Isn't the drunk sawbones a cliché in these parts?'

'Clichés got reasons, I figure, but in this case Doc Butler never met a liquor he didn't cotton to.'

'I'll be back to talk to you again at some point, Marshal. . . ?'

'Hooper. And make sure you bring the little lady with you.' The lawdog cast Tootie another lascivious glance.

'Marshal, I swear you look at me that way again and you'll be needin' the doc to pull your badge out of your flop chute.' Tootie smiled demurely, then reined around. Jim Hannigan chuckled under his breath then followed suit.

The marshal watched them go, anger washing across his face. A ten-count later, he vanished into his office.

'There's a hotel yonder.' Hannigan ducked his chin towards the building. 'Let's set up there until it's time to talk to the doc.'

Tootie nodded. 'It's gonna take a week of baths to wash that skunk's gaze off of me.'

Hannigan grinned. 'All I could do not to shoot

35

one of his ears off.'

Tootie nodded. 'I was thinking about something lower than his ears.'

'He was lying.' Hannigan reined up in front of the hotel, glanced at Tootie.

She brought her own mount to a halt and eyed him. 'But about what? About Deadwood being dead or about the killing in general? I reckon he might have an idea who did it.'

'Got the same notion.' He dismounted, then tethered his roan to the rail. Tootie jumped from the saddle, looped her reins about the rail, then stretched her arms and legs.

'I might've seen him before, but I can't recollect where. Getting to be a habit.'

He raised an eyebrow. 'It'll come to you.'

They stepped onto the boardwalk, then crossed to the door. Hannigan opened it and gestured for Tootie to go first. He closed the door behind them.

A frail-looking man scurried from the back room at the clanging of the bell above the door. The lobby was sparse, the carpet worn and dusty, the few pieces of furniture having seen better days.

'Lookin' for a room?' the man asked, as they reached the desk. He peered up at them from beneath a green visor.

'One week to start.' Hannigan pulled a wad of greenbacks from his pocket. He peeled off a number of bills and tossed them onto the counter.

The clerk turned a register around and shoved it towards him. 'Will that be one room, or two?' He glanced at Tootie, who smiled.

'That'll be one,' she said.

'I see,' the clerk said. 'Well, I'll have to charge double for that.' The man eyed the greenbacks Hannigan was returning to his pocket.

The manhunter caught the man's gaze. 'That'd be plain robbery, my friend.'

'Fella's gotta eat.'

Hannigan frowned, pulled the roll back out, then tossed more bills onto the counter. 'Reckon you'll be tallowed by this time next week, then.'

The clerk grinned and passed Hannigan a key. 'Room six, upstairs.'

Once upstairs Hannigan located room six and unlocked the door. The room was dingy, with just a worn bed covered with sheets that looked years old, a bureau atop which sat a steel basin and an empty pitcher, a nightstand with a lantern, and a rickety chair in a corner. Tootie followed Hannigan into the room, glancing about in disgust. She closed the door and pressed her back against it.

'Lovely,' she whispered.

Hannigan nodded and stamped on a roach that skittered from beneath the bed.

'We best get our gear, then grab a bite at the café before we question the doc. We hit the trail early this morning.'

She grinned. 'I've got a better idea.' Her fingers went to the buttons of her blouse and she slowly began to undo them.

Hannigan couldn't stop a foolish grin from spreading across his lips and shivers from frolicking along his spine. She slipped off her top, then

37

whisked the hat from her head and flung it to the chair.

'Hell, I wasn't hungry anyhow. . . .' he said and she giggled.

CHAPTER THREE

Three hours later Hannigan wondered if he'd ever walk straight again, but felt more satisfied and alive than any man had a right to be. Each time he lay with her was better than the time before. She possessed some kind of magic, he reckoned, the magic over men that made women the stronger sex, as well as the lovelier.

Tootie del Pelado was everything a man could ever hope to find and a dark suspicion taunted him that he didn't really deserve her, that a man such as he was destined to die alone and he would one day wake up to find he'd no more than dreamed her.

Half an hour more and they had transferred their gear to the room: saddlebags, Winchester, bedrolls. After boarding their mounts at the over-priced livery, they walked along the boardwalk towards the sawbones's office.

Tootie glanced at him with a smile that made butterflies flutter through his belly. Raw emotion radiated from her mahogany eyes, emotion that made him uncomfortable yet fulfilled at the same time.

Worry followed, worry that he'd lose her on one of their missions. Worry that one of his enemies would track them down and strike at her to get at him.

He told himself that that was the lot he'd accepted the moment he'd taken her to his bed, but the notion did little to ease his concerns.

A wooden sign sporting the name Doctor Thaddeus Butler hung above the door to the sawbones's office, which was catty-corner to Main Street and Lariat. They entered the office, were immediately hit with some medicinal scent and another that he pegged as old gin. The reception room was small, containing a few chairs lined against a wall and a small desk angled into a corner. Dusty sunlight arced through grimy windowpanes.

A man shambled out from the back room, which Hannigan presumed was the examination area. Dark pouches nested beneath his eyes and a haggard expression made his face droop like a hound dog's. His steely hair, tousled, hung over his forehead. His frame was stooped, though he appeared just a shade past forty.

'We ain't open yet,' the man said, annoyance in his tone.

'You Doc Butler?' Hannigan asked, stepping deeper into the room.

'Who wants to know?' The man appeared perturbed at nothing in particular, his tone challenging. Hannigan wondered if everybody in this town lived that way.

'Jim Hannigan. I came to ask you some questions

about James Deadwood.'

The man cocked an eyebrow, a dark glint coming into his eyes. He glanced at Tootie. 'And who's this?'

'Angela del Pelado,' Tootie answered. 'I'm his partner.'

'Reckon you are,' the doc said with a note of sarcasm. He looked back to the manhunter. 'Hannigan . . . you that bounty fella?'

Jim nodded. 'Some folks call me that.'

'Why do you want to know about Deadwood? He a friend of yours?'

'Wouldn't call him that. I was sent to make sure he was dead.'

The doc laughed, then held his head, a pained expression jumping onto his face.

'Dead as dead could be.'

'You examined him, determined cause of death?'

The sawbones nodded. 'Yep, sure did. Had enough bullet holes in him to kill twenty men. Whoever shot him sure had it out for the fella.'

'You're sure it was Deadwood?'

The doc's brow cinched. 'Sure I'm sure! What the hell kind of question is that?'

Hannigan ignored the query. 'He buried in town?'

The doc hesitated and Hannigan caught something in the man's eyes he damn well didn't care for – the same look of a lie he'd seen in Hooper's.

'Cemetery just outside of town. 'Cept it won't do you no good to dig him up, if that's what you got a notion to do.'

The sawbones had nailed Hannigan's thought dead on. 'Why's that?'

'Deadwood was part Apache. Figured he'd want an Apache burial, so we burned him first.'

'Burned him?' Surprise washed across Tootie's face.

'Seemed only right to honor tradition,' the doc said.

Hannigan tipped a finger to his hat. 'Reckon that tells me what I wanted to know.'

The manhunter turned and walked to the door. Tootie, looking puzzled, followed. Once they were outside and heading along the boardwalk she grabbed Hannigan's arm.

'Why'd you leave so quick? I got the notion he was lying.'

Jim nodded. 'Same as the marshal.'

'Shouldn't we have pressed him more?'

'Wouldn't do any good at this point. I want to confirm something 'fore I go pressing anyone.'

She peered at him. 'Where we going?'

'*I'm* going to the cemetery. You're going back to the hotel.'

'You a wagering man?' A smug expression came to her lips.

He frowned. 'Not normally.'

'Good, because it's a fool's bet against me coming with you.'

He let out a heavy sigh and didn't bother to argue.

The cemetery was located about a hundred yards out of town, in a hilly section surrounded by trees exposed to wind gusts that swooped down from the mountains. Most of the leaves had deserted their branches and covered the ground in a brittle brown carpet. An iron fence rimmed the cemetery, which held rows of thin stones and wooden markers. A shack that Hannigan hoped housed the groundskeeper's tools stood near the back. He spotted no sign of anyone, and likely a town like Autumn Pass wouldn't bother with a full-time keeper, merely one hired when needed, which probably was often.

Hannigan pushed open the gate; it creaked like the sound of a dying cat. The noise rode his nerves. He wasn't much for cemeteries and what he planned to do for the second time in about a month's period was not a task he relished.

'This is getting to be a sorry habit,' he muttered.

'What is?' Tootie asked, following him towards the shack.

'Diggin' up corpses.' The thought of desecrating a grave made his belly twist.

She nodded. 'Let's hope this grave's as empty as the last one.'

'Got a feeling that won't be the case.'

He reached the shack, opened the door, and located a shovel. Tootie grabbed a second digger, then trailed Hannigan as he searched the stones and markers for Deadwood's name.

Two aisles over, he found a thin stone with the gunfighter's name chiseled into it.

Frowning, he glanced at Tootie, then began to dig. The earth was still soft.

Tootie's help made the task go faster than on the previous time in Hollow Pass when, alone, he'd exhumed Trip Matterly's coffin, only to find it empty. He was positive a body lay in this grave, but whose?

With the sound of a hollow thud, he knew he had hit the coffin. The casket wasn't anywhere near as far down as he expected it to be, no more than three feet. He scraped the dirt from the top and dug around the box so he'd have no trouble lifting the lid.

After they'd exposed the ornate top, Tootie jumped out of the hole and Hannigan tossed his shovel aside. He stood on a lip he had dug in the ground beside the coffin, then doubled and gripped the lid. It came up with a rain of soil and no creaking, for which he was thankful

'Jesus!' Tootie turned away and covered her mouth with her hand.

'Sure as hell ain't a pretty sight. . . .' he mumbled.

The horrid odor of burnt flesh and decay wafted from within the coffin. Hannigan flinched, having all he could do to look at the charred corpse.

'They burned him, all right,' Tootie said, still looking away from the corpse.

'That they did,' Hannigan whispered.

'Is it him? Is it Deadwood?'

Hannigan forced himself to examine the grisly remains more closely. 'Size and general build looks right, from what I recollect. Deadwood was tall, six-four, at least. This fella's about that but I can't make out any features. His face is too charred.'

A round black object caught his attention and, against his revulsion, he pulled a blackened pocket-watch from the corpse. He rubbed the watch against the dirt, clearing away some of the soot to reveal an inscription on the back: In honorarium: James Deadwood.

Hannigan glanced up at Tootie, who stared out at the mountains. 'Watch's inscription says it belongs to Deadwood.'

She nodded.

Hannigan placed the watch back on the corpse, then closed the lid and climbed from the grave. Queasy, he reckoned that odor would likely stay in his memory for a hell of a lot longer than he cared to think about.

'Then our job's done here?' Tootie said, looking back to him now that the lid was closed.

'Reckon it ain't.'

Her brow cinched with confusion. 'You said that's him. What's left to do?'

'I said the size and build was right. Didn't say it was him.'

'But there isn't any other way to tell it's him and the watch—'

'The watch could have been planted.'

Tootie frowned. 'But the doc said Deadwood was part Apache and they burned their dead.'

'That's what he said.' Jim grabbed the shovel and began to pile dirt into the grave. 'But this body was burned, not cremated.'

Tootie fetched her own shovel and helped. 'You're leaving something out. What is it?' She glanced at him, face serious.

He nodded. 'Some Indians cremate their dead. They don't just burn off the features. Not Apache; they bury their dead in crevices.'

'So you're saying. . . ?'

'Someone burned that man on purpose. That makes me question things.' He shrugged. 'That body may well belong to Deadwood. Maybe somebody just had a gruesome grudge. That might be what the doc and marshal are trying to cover up.'

'Or maybe someone wanted to make the body unrecognizable. . . .' Tootie said as she hurled another shovel of dirt into the grave.

'Which leads right back to the doc or marshal again.'

'If it isn't Deadwood, or even if it is, how are we going to prove it?'

'That's a question to be answered . . .' He gave her a grim expression. 'One thing I know, I don't like a damn thing I've seen since we came to this town. I reckon someone in Autumn Pass has answers and I ain't about to leave until I get them.'

Marshal Hooper scooped his hat from his head as he crossed the floor to the stairs leading to the Wild Bull saloon's upper level. The place was fairly quiet this time of afternoon, but men would start pouring in soon and he wanted to be out of the drinkerie before that happened.

He climbed the stairs, the effort taxing him more than it should have. He wondered if his heart wasn't just going to give up sometime soon. He was too damn fat, that he knew, and anything resembling real physical work repulsed him, 'less it was bedding whores, which he considered worth the effort. If he was going to go out he would do it with a goddamn smile on his face.

By the time he reached the top step sweat ran freely down his face and from beneath his arms. His breath huffed out. His heart thudded but he reckoned some of that might have been from the anxiety of his having to come here to relate the news of that manhunter's arrival. It was a damn bad thing that fella was in Autumn Pass.

The marshal reached room four and glanced behind him at the gloomy hallway to make sure no one had followed him. They still had to be careful for another week.

He eased open the door, then stepped into the room. Dark shades, drawn, kept the room in virtual darkness. It took a moment for his eyes to adjust. He spotted the dim outlines of a bed, nightstand and the bureau against the wall. A sliver of late-afternoon daylight ran along either side of the shade.

He went to the bureau and pounded a fist against the wall beside it, then ambled to the bed and sat on the edge, thankful to take the weight off his feet.

Waiting in the darkened room gave him the willies. He wished the bastard would hurry up before he sweat himself plumb dry.

A thin scraping sounded. The marshal's head jerked towards the wall, to a space beside the bureau. Someone now stood in the room with him;

he could just make out the outline of human shape.

'What is it?' a voice came, a harsh whisper of a thing that gave him a shiver.

'We got trouble,' the marshal said, mopping sweat from his brow with a shirt sleeve.

'Trouble? Don't reckon I paid for trouble.'

'Man named Hannigan. . . .'

'Oh, Christ,' the whisperer said, following it with a heavy sigh.

'He was asking questions about James Deadwood, too. Think he plans to question the doc. He asked me who viewed the body.'

'And you told him, you dumb bastard?'

'What the hell was I s'posed to do? I didn't expect no one like him to come sniffin' around. That never happened before.'

'He's dangerous as hell.'

'You think I don't know that? He's got some woman with him, too.'

'Who is she?'

The marshal shook his head. 'No idea. But she's a tough gal, I could tell. Pretty one, too.'

'Keep your pecker in your pants where she's concerned, Edgecomb.'

'You shouldn't call me that.' The marshal stood. 'Just thought you should know.'

'Watch him. He gets close to anything you tell me. Taking care of him won't be easy.'

Marshal Hooper nodded and fingered the rim of his hat, then went to the door. He peered behind him, then stepped out into the hallway. After shutting the door he burst out in another round of the

sweats. Maybe it was time to arrange a disappearance for himself, before Hannigan got too close
and did it for real.

CHAPTER FOUR

The Wild Bull saloon had hit full swing by the time Tootie pushed through the batwings. She'd dressed in a red-sateen bodice and frilly skirt, which she'd kept wrapped in her bedroll. Her blue-black hair hung straight over her shoulders. She hadn't bothered having her make-up supplies shipped since Hannigan had told her before leaving she wouldn't need them for the simple day-or-two mission. Although he hadn't explained exactly what the mission would be when they left Denver, she had tucked away the bargal outfit just in case she needed it, along with a couple other tools of her trade, such as her derringer.

A small smile filtered onto her lips. Hannigan hadn't been particularly happy when he discovered she had brought the get-up, nor when she'd told him she was going to try the saloon for information. All his arguments about Autumn Pass being a rough town and the job becoming dangerous now that it had turned into more than just the simple identification of a dead gunslinger had fallen on deaf ears.

She reckoned there was only one way he could

get her to stop risking her neck and that was by settling down somewhere and leaving the business. But she wouldn't bring that up to him, at least not at this point. She preferred he came to it on his own. Menfolk had to think it was their idea or they'd resent it at some future point.

Standing just inside the doors, she looked over the room, studying the rowdy crowd and handful of whores making their rounds. Her gaze settled briefly on the mezzanine balcony, probing its shadowy expanse, then dropped back to the barroom proper. A haze of Durham smoke clouded the room and stung her nostrils. She heard more vulgar words in the space of a few moments than any gal should have heard in a lifetime. She picked out a number of hardcases, all involved in drinking or card-playing. This town was a respite for them and unless provoked they would likely keep to themselves. Of course, what it took to provoke some of them often amounted to little more than a sideways glance.

She stepped down into the room, assessing each whore in turn, selecting one who she thought might prove likely to talk. They all appeared a tough lot, most with faces like mules and shoulders near as wide as a man's. Only one had any looks and that was the gal the marshal had shoved off his lap earlier.

Tootie decided that gal would be the best one to start with. She might have an axe to grind after the way that lawdog had treated her, and men – even crooked lawmen – whispered things to women who whispered to them.

She threaded her way through the crowd, fending off two attempts to grab her posterior and another to squeeze something a bit higher on her person.

The girl – and she was a girl, now that Tootie got a closer look at her, no more than sixteen or seventeen, despite the heavy pancake she'd plastered on her face – looked up at her as she approached. Annalea was her name, if Tootie recollected right.

Annalea flicked her auburn hair back with a jerky movement of her head, then started to walk away, obviously recognizing Tootie and having little desire for a second encounter.

Tootie grabbed the young woman's arm and swung her around. A fierce look that should never have tainted one so young flashed across the girl's face. Her dull blue eyes showed evidence of some sort of drug, likely laudanum, and most of her underdeveloped bosom was on display in a peek-a-boo blouse.

'I just want to talk to you a minute,' Tootie said, as the girl jerked her arm free.

'Ain't no reason for you to be talkin' to me.' The girl folded her arms, eyes narrowing, defiant. 'I recollect you from earlier today and you'll jest get me in trouble with that fat bastard lawdog.' The girl's eyes narrowed. 'You didn't look like no whore then, though.'

Tootie tried a smile. 'Just wanted to say I'm sorry.'

The girl's face softened a fraction. 'For what?'

'For the way that horrible marshal treated you. A

lady deserves more respect than that.'

The girl studied her, apparently deciding she was sincere, though not entirely trusting as to why. Tootie reckoned she was helped by whatever drug was obscuring the girl's powers of reason.

'Weren't your fault. He's a bastard through and through. Always treats me that way.'

'Why do you put up with it? I'd blow his oysters clean to Galveston, if I were you.'

The girl's shoulders sagged, and she looked suddenly older than her years. A peculiar sadness crept into her eyes, the same emotion Tootie had glimpsed earlier, though deeper. Tootie felt suddenly a little guilty about mining her for information.

'He pays better'n any of the fellas in here. I reckon a smelly old sonofabitch like that would have to, else no gal would want to touch his dirty pecker.'

Tootie cringed inside, but didn't let it show on her face. 'You got a home anywhere, someplace else you could go to get away from him, from . . . this?' She ducked her chin at the crowded room.

The girl laughed. 'What're you, girly, some sort of do-gooder?' Annalea studied her again. 'You really *don't* look like no whore, you know. You're too pretty and that fella you rode in with don't look like the type to be sellin' you. You ain't fixin' to work here, are you?' A glint of jealousy and worry jumped into the girl's eyes.

Tootie shook her head. 'Just passin' through. You ain't answered my question.'

The girl frowned. 'I got nowhere else to go. My folks was kilt when I was a young'n. No life for a girl after that, not in these parts.'

A surge of empathy went through Tootie. Her own life might well have turned out this way under other circumstances – if she had been less driven to bring down the men who had taken so much from her. She made a decision then, one that might risk her chance of getting information from the girl, but one she needed to make for her own conscience.

'That fella I rode in with, he's staying at the hotel. His name is Jim Hannigan. He can help you. You decide you want out of this life you go to him and tell him Tootie sent you. The decision's one *you* have to make, though.'

Annalea laughed, half as if she thought Tootie was making some sort of joke at her expense and half that said she'd resigned herself to being nothing more than she was now.

'Can't trust no fella, sugar. They're all the same. They only want what's 'twixt your legs.'

Tootie shook her head. 'He's a good man. He ain't like the rest.'

The girl frowned. 'Thank you kindly, but I reckon my future's writ.'

Tootie swallowed as a knot of emotion lodged in her throat. She'd done all she could do under the circumstances. 'Heard you had a killin' here 'bout a week back.'

The girl laughed, but her voice carried a melancholy edge it hadn't before.

'Famous gunslinger got his ticket punched. Was in all the papers. Everybody was talkin' 'bout it for a few days, then they went back to hell as usual.'

'You know anything about it?'

A flicker of suspicion passed across the girl's eyes, but in her condition she couldn't retain it. 'Not so much. Tilda led him upstairs to room four and somebody filled him full of lead. Then Tilda got herself kilt the next day. Stupid bitch. Some things a gal shouldn't do for money, I reckon, and that's get involved with some of the lowly types who come in here.'

'You think one of those types killed that fella?'

Annalea shrugged. 'Reckon. Who else? Plenty of fellas lookin' to kill a famous gunslinger.'

'You see the body?'

'Hell, no! I got me better to do than go 'round lookin' at dead fellas.'

'No one saw who did it, then?'

'Not to my recollection. Somehow they got out, though Christ on a crutch I can't see how. No outside stairway. Would have had to jump out the winder in the room and it's a drop.'

Tootie frowned, frustration getting to her a bit more because of her concern for the girl. She had the urge to slap Annalea for making this choice. Times like these, she wished she could just say to hell with the case and ride out with Hannigan into a different life, a peaceful life. Maybe she'd seen enough pain and death in her nineteen years.

'You recollect what I said about that man.' Tootie touched the girl's shoulder. 'Offer's open anytime.'

Annalea's eyes watered and she sniffled, then quickly hid any sign of weakness with a defiant set of her features. 'Like I said, can't trust no man.'

Tootie gave her a grim smile and started to turn, figuring her next mark would have to be the saloon-keep, or maybe one of the harder gals.

'You could talk to his daughter. . . .' Annalea said, as if she suddenly didn't want Tootie to leave.

Tootie turned back to her. 'His daughter?'

'She came in two days after he got kilt. Started working at the dress-shop the day after that. She don't look so much like a gunfighter's daughter, though.'

'What's she look like?'

'One of us, maybe. She dresses nice, like she's all sugar and spice when folks are lookin', but I reckon you can't hide what you are, can you?'

'But you can change it. . . .' She gave the girl a warm smile that was chopped short as a shriek came from one of the other bargirls.

Tootie's gaze snapped towards the screamer, saw her staring up at the mezzanine. Tootie's attention swung upwards, catching a glimpse of the figure of a man. The figure, tall, dark, stepped back into the shadows, frock-coat whisking like a flag in a breeze. Had she caught a glimpse of his face, the dark eyes that seemed to bore into her soul even from that distance? Or had her mind merely filled in the features, based on her reaction to Hannigan's tintype and digging up Deadwood's grave earlier in the day?

The barroom went silent, except for the girl's

shrieks. A hardcase jumped up and slapped her quiet.

'What the hell?' a cowboy said, looking up.

'A goddamn spook!' the bargirl said, voice high-pitched, laced with hysteria. 'Was that Deadwood fella, I swear it was! A goddamn dead man, it was, standing right there a'lookin' down at us.'

As if in response a whispered laugh came from the darkness of the mezzanine and drifted downward. Three men jumped out of their chairs and left the saloon, the looks on their faces saying they'd drink with owlhoots and whores but spooks were out of the question.

Tootie stood frozen, unable even to blink. Something about that figure, that man in Hannigan's tintype, gripped her composure, sent chills through her body. Gooseflesh rose on her bare shoulders and arms.

'Was that a spook?' Annalea suddenly asked beside her, startling Tootie from her spell.

Tootie shook her head, mumbled, 'No such things.' She forced herself to move, hand slipping into the top of her bodice and bringing out a derringer.

No one else made a move to go up the stairs and investigate whoever had been standing there, whoever's ghostly laugh still seemed to echo through the saloon.

She reached the stairs, legs shakier than she was used to, palms damp. This kind of fear wasn't like her. She ran towards trouble, not away from it.

The climb felt like a hundred miles of rough trail

and she noticed her gun hand shaking.

Get hold of yourself, Tootie. No such things as spooks. . . .

But there was some other terror, something buried deep within her the sight of that man unearthed. She couldn't explain it, couldn't understand it, but she felt it plain as day.

Who the hell are you, James Deadwood?

She reached the landing, ran along it, gun raised, eyes searching each shadow in case he lay in wait. The mezzanine was empty, whoever had been there gone.

In the hall, she went to a wall lantern and turned the flame high. The hallway was empty. Four doors, two to either side, lay before her. She went to the first, threw it open. The room was lit by a lantern on a nightstand, but deserted. She entered the room, grabbed the lantern, then returned to the hallway.

The next two rooms proved to be dark, but empty.

That left room four. Her heart started to pound and she tried to suppress it without much luck. He had to be in that room and she could not afford to freeze again. She turned the glass knob with her lantern hand, keeping the derringer ready in her other. The door swung inward with a thin creak.

A gentle thump sounded as the door hit the wall, telling her no one lurked behind it, waiting to ambush her.

The room was dark and as she stepped across the threshold, she held the lantern before her. She squeezed the derringer in her other hand, ready to trigger an instant shot.

'You best step out where I can see you, you sono-fabitch!' She struggled to keep her voice steady. 'You think I won't blow your head off you got another think comin'.'

Silence. She listened, ears straining for any hint of an inhaled breath, the slightest rustle of clothing.

Nothing.

Except her banging heart and the throb of her pulse in her ears.

She swung the lantern about the room, seeing a bed, nightstand and bureau, but nothing else. The room was empty.

'Maybe you really are a ghost. . . .' she whispered.

For one of the few times in her life she felt like running as fast and as far as her legs would carry her.

CHAPTER FIVE

Jim Hannigan decided he'd given Tootie enough time to question bargirls at the saloon. Now it was his turn, whether she liked it or not. He wasn't exactly checking up on her, making sure she was safe, after all. He was just doing his job.

And you think she'll believe that?

He uttered a laugh under his breath as he stepped from the hotel and headed to the saloon. He reckoned he didn't even have to ask that question, but since she had given him no choice in her course of action the least he could do was return the favor.

As he reached the saloon two men burst through the batwings. They shoved past him, fear scrawled across their faces, which were as white as November snow. They hit the street running, and didn't look back.

'What the hell was that about?' Hannigan mumbled, then pushed through the doors. The place was eerily quiet for a saloon. Patrons stared up at a shadowy mezzanine, eyes wide, mouths agape. One bargirl, looking flushed, sat in a chair, fanning herself with a wad of greenbacks.

Hannigan took the three steps to the barroom proper and approached one of the men who was looking up at the mezzanine.

'What the hell's going on?' he asked, his own gaze traveling upward.

'Lidia saw a spook standing up there. Think it was that Deadwood fella's ghost.'

Hannigan glanced at the cowboy, wondering whether the man was drunk or putting him on, but when he saw the fear in the man's eyes he decided it was no joke. 'Ghost? No such animal.'

The man shook his head. 'You wouldn't say that iffen you'da seen him. Big as life, laughin' at us like the Devil's coyote.'

Hannigan's brow cinched. 'Anybody chase after this ghost?'

The man nodded. 'Some bargal. Ain't never seen her before.'

'Oh, Christ,' Hannigan muttered, knowing exactly who had gone up there.

His hand went to the snub-nosed Peacemaker at his hip. He drew the weapon and went to the stairs. He took them in bounds, caution thrown to the wind by worry over Tootie. As he reached the top he scanned the shadows, then he scuttled along the mezzanine to the hallway. The hallway was deserted but the door to the fourth room was open, light coming from within, spilling out across the threadbare carpet in jittery specters.

Flanking the wall, he made his way down the hall, gun raised to his chin. At the door, he stopped, edged around, gun ready. He saw Tootie, standing in the room holding a lantern and derringer, but no one else.

'Tootie?'

She spun, a startled gasp escaping her lips, fear on her face. He didn't see that emotion on her often and he didn't care for it a lick.

'Jim. . . .' She lowered the derringer.

'What happened?'

'There was a man . . . standing on the balcony. He came up here but he's . . . gone.'

'Gone?' Hannigan stepped into the room, glancing at its sparse furnishings.

Tootie tucked the derringer into her bodice and shuddered. 'He must have come this way but every room is empty and all the windows are closed. He couldn't have gotten away . . . but he did.'

'Some fella said it was a spook.'

The look on her face told him she was thinking it damn well might have been. 'A bargirl started shrieking, looking up. I looked up to see a fella stepping back into the shadows, but I'm not sure I got a good look.'

'Was it Deadwood?'

She licked her lips, shook her head slightly. 'I . . . can't say for sure. Might have been. Think it was; least, I had his face in my head when I saw the figure. But it might have been 'cause I was expecting it, 'cause I saw your picture.'

Hannigan holstered his gun and stepped over to her, touching her shoulder. 'You all right?'

'I reckon. I swear, Jim, I saw someone and he

couldn't have gotten away. I came right up after him. There's no way out.'

'But he ain't here now?'

She shook her head. 'I'm not loco. I *did* see someone.'

'Folks in the barroom saw him, too, but where the hell did he go?'

'You think he might have been a. . . .'

He laughed. 'I don't believe in such.'

She nodded. 'I don't either, but mighty peculiar him just vanishing that way, isn't it?'

'Gotta be an explanation for it. I'm not ready to accept ghosts and goblins.' Hannigan's gaze skipped about the room again.

'This is the room where it happened, according to Annalea,' Tootie said. 'Deadwood was killed in here.'

'There'd be signs of it, then.' Hannigan took the lantern from Tootie's grip. He knelt, studying the worn floorboards. He spotted two small stains in the wood, dark brown. 'Blood.'

Tootie nodded. 'Marshal said he was shot.'

'Mmm, except there ain't enough.'

'Enough what?'

'Enough blood. Two small stains, yet somebody filled Deadwood full of holes. You might expect more bleeding.' His gaze locked on a hole in the floor and he set the lantern beside it. He unsheathed the Bowie knife at his boot and with its tip pried at the hole. A moment later he extricated a mangled slug. He examined it, then dropped it into a pocket and sheathed his knife.

'What'd you find?' Tootie asked, bending over him, voice calmer now.

He gazed up at her, forearm across his knee. 'A bullet that went through a body and buried itself in the floor, from the looks of it.'

'So?' She straightened, wrapping her arms about herself.

'So whoever was shot with it was lying on the floor at the time, not standing.'

'Maybe they shot him a few times after he fell, just to make sure.'

He stood, face grim. 'Maybe. But I reckon they might've put it in his head if that were the case, and there'd sure as hell be a bigger mess here than two small stains.'

She sighed. 'Does it matter? Reckon it proves there was a dead man in this room.'

'Reckon it does, but it doesn't prove it was Deadwood. No way to tell, even if there had been a lot of blood, but I don't like what I'm seein'. Too many pieces that alone might not mean a thing, but together might point to something going on beyond the killing of a famous gunslinger.'

'And now this ghost thing.'

'And now this ghost thing.' He picked up the lantern, then set it on the nightstand. 'You get anything out of anyone?'

She shook her head as they headed to the door, then out into the hallway. 'Nothing useful. 'Cept that girl, Annalea, the one the marshal had on his fat lap earlier. . . .'

'What about her?'

'She doesn't belong doin' what she's doin'.'

He peered at her. 'You developin' a social conscience?'

She grinned. 'I could have been a nun, I ever tell you that?'

'Reckon I'm glad that ain't a path you chose to follow.'

They went down the stairs, pausing at the bottom. The ghost had apparently been forgotten, as men had gone back to playing poker, drinking, and fondling women. The marshal stood a few feet from the stairs, eyeing them.

'Spook-hunting, now, Mr Hannigan?' the marshal asked. 'Could be a new profession for ya. Might keep you from ending up like that other gunslinger.'

Hannigan caught a concealed threat in the man's tone but wasn't much in the mood to spar with him. 'Upstairs was empty. You got any notion how a man could go up there and vanish?'

The marshal smiled, an ugly expression. 'Spooks . . . they got a habit of doin' that, I'm told.'

'You're a damn lot of help.' Hannigan frowned and made a move to step past the man.

'Reckon I try my best,' the marshal said. 'Annalea, we got business – upstairs!'

A few feet away the young bargirl jolted. Hannigan saw Tootie's features wash with anger. Annalea glanced at Tootie, a strange expression of sadness darkening her face. Her head dropped as the marshal went to her and took her by the hand, then led her towards the stairs. She gave Tootie another glance that held almost an apology before heading upstairs with him.

'She's in for a rough night . . .' Hannigan said. 'I could go pull her out.'

Tootie shook her head, guilt in her mahogany eyes. 'No, she has to decide that for herself or it'll just be another town, another fella like Hooper.'

Hannigan nodded as they went towards the batwings. 'You're wise beyond your years, Miss del Pelado. . . .'

'I see riders comin'!' the little dark-haired girl yelled, twisting her head to look back at her parents and brother, who had just entered the small parlor. The little girl knelt atop a cedar chest pushed against the wall beneath the window. A little past her sixth birthday, she was dressed in a tattered dress she had put on in anticipation of going fishing with her older brother, Alejandro. She'd promised him she wouldn't fall into the river this time and he'd managed to persuade her parents to give her another chance. But any excitement she'd felt a moment before faded at the sight of those two men riding hell-bent for the small ranch house. She couldn't have told why; it was just some inner fear that crawled up and took hold of her mind. They were bad men, she knew it. Only bad men would come riding in that way and no one came to the del Pelado farm unless they brought trouble. One thing she had learned early: folks in these parts didn't like Mexicans and their half-breed children.

A chill blew through her, like a frosty autumn

breeze. She shivered.

'Who'd be ridin' out this way?' her father asked, coming up beside her and peering through the window. His dark-brown eyes narrowed and he smelled of the cornflour he'd been grinding for tortillas. She loved that scent; it was part of who he was, his heritage – *her* heritage, one of which he'd taught her to be proud.

She wanted to beg him not to let those men see him at the window, but she couldn't think of any real reason they shouldn't be kindly towards the strangers, other than the chill freezing her innards.

'Who are they, Juan?' asked her mother, wiping her hands of her blue-flower print apron. Her mother was a pretty blonde woman, the prettiest in the whole Territory, Tootie reckoned. Her creamy complexion and dainty features gave her an elegant beauty that made Tootie wish she hadn't taken after her father's side. Her mother was like the little porcelain doll her grandmother had handed down to her, something to be put on a shelf and admired. The same beauty that drove many of the folks in town to hate the fact that Allison del Pelado had married what she'd heard them call a chilli-eater.

Her father shook his head. 'Can't tell from here, but they're ridin' like their tails were lit afire.'

'Move, nincompoop,' Alejandro said, jostling Tootie aside so he could see out the window. Tootie elbowed him and he scowled at her.

'Watch your tongue, *niño*,' Juan said, tone only mildly scolding. Whatever Tootie felt, she reckoned her pa felt it too, because worry bled into his voice.

'Storm's comin'. . . .' Alejandro said, peering out at the men, who were much closer now.

'What're you talkin' about, Alejandro?' asked his mother, stepping deeper into the room. 'There's not a cloud in the sky.'

The ten-year-old boy glanced back at his mother. 'Not a rainstorm, those men. They're runnin' from somethin', else they wouldn't have come here, and they wouldn't be ridin' so fast. No one ever comes out to the chilli-eaters' farm.' The last came with a note of bitterness and Tootie knew her brother was fed up with the taunts from schoolkids, and maybe fed up with protecting her from the daily abuse fostered upon her by schoolmates intolerant of her mixed breeding.

Juan gave his son a scolding look. 'I've told you about using that name. Some folks can't help their small-mindedness. Next time it's the switch.'

Alejandro's lips tightened into a frown and anger lashed at his dark eyes, but he went quiet.

'Go to your room, children,' her mother said. 'Don't come out 'til those men are gone.'

Tootie looked back at her mother, but saw that the expression on her face brooked no argument.

'I don't want to—' Alejandro began.

'Do it!' Juan snapped, casting him a stern look. 'Now!'

Both children scooted from the window and went to the room off the parlor. Tootie left the door ajar, then pressed her face to the opening and watched. Alejandro poised above her, doing the same.

She heard the horses come to a stop, then came

a moment of silence before a heavy pounding banged against the door.

'Open up, we know you're in there!' came a harsh voice through the door. 'We saw ya at the window.'

'What do you want?' her father called out. He moved towards the wall, where pegs held a Winchester.

The door careened inward. A man stood there, lingering on the threshold, a man taller than any Tootie had ever seen, with long hair the color of saddle leather. But it wasn't his height that froze her. It was the eyes glaring from beneath the battered hat. Dark eyes, cruel eyes, eyes that could pierce right through to your soul. Those eyes were the eyes of death.

The man suddenly had a gun in his hand, drawing it so fast it might have just appeared there by magic. 'I wouldn't iffen I were you, Pedro,' the man said, and her father stopped a few feet short of the Winchester. He would never reach the rifle before the man gunned him down.

The man stepped into the house, boots thudding on the floorboards, Tootie's heart pounding in rhythm.

'He's a giant. . . .' Alejandro whispered.

'He's the Devil,' Tootie said, for the first time in her young life feeling such a terrible fear that she worried she would just explode with it.

'Come on out here, children.' The man swung the gun towards the bedroom door and Tootie shuddered. Alejandro glanced at her, fear on his face, and she didn't move. 'Now! I ain't a man known for my patience.'

'Leave them be!' her mother said.

The man laughed. 'Tell them to come on out here, or I'll kill their pa.'

Tootie acted then, without thought, without hesitation. She yanked open the door, nearly banging Alejandro, who jumped back just in time, in the face. She strode out into the parlor, unable to take her eyes from the man's cruel gaze, but defiant just the same.

'Sit on the sofa,' he ordered. Both children went to it and sat on the edge.

'What do you want here?' her pa asked, worry over his family plain in his eyes. 'We are poor farmers. We have nothing you could want.'

Another man stepped in behind the first and went to the window, peered out. He was a wiry type, nearly a foot shorter than the first, dressed in a stained shirt and dirty trousers.

'See anyone?' asked the tall man.

The man at the window shook his head. 'No sign of 'em. Reckon we got away clean.'

'All the same, keep an eye out. They might take the notion we came this way.' The man kicked the door shut, peered at the two children, then at Juan del Pelado. 'Your hospitality's what we want. We need a place to hole up for a few hours. Seems the local law got a bit peeled we tried to take something that didn't exactly belong to us. We settled for escaping with our lives. Your ranch just happened to be on our way out.'

'Please, just leave us be. . . .' her father said, the worry in his tone growing stronger.

The man's dark eyes narrowed as they settled on her mother, whose face had gone white. '*You* – get in the kitchen and make us some coffee. I hear anything other than a pot brewin' and you'll wish to hell I hadn't.'

Her mother shot a worried glance at her father, then backed into the kitchen.

The man at the window looked over to his partner, grinning. 'She sure is a pretty little filly, ain't she? You think I could—'

'No,' the taller man answered, then smiled. 'But I will. You watch them.'

The man at the window clearly didn't like that arrangement but didn't appear inclined to challenge the other's authority.

The taller man moved back, aim still locked on Juan, then vanished into the kitchen. The hardcase at the window straightened and kept his gaze on her pa.

Her father's face grew redder by the second, anger replacing worry.

From the kitchen the sound of her mother's startled yelp, then the banging of pots sent a chill down Tootie's back.

'No!' came her mother's voice, pleading. 'Leave me be, please, don't. . . .'

'Come on, you dumb bitch!' she heard the man rasp. Tootie looked to her father, hoping, praying he could somehow stop what was happening. She perched on the edge of the sofa, ready to spring for the kitchen, feeling more helpless than when she had fallen into the river.

Fury crossed her father's features and he whirled, lunged towards the kitchen.

The man at the window grabbed the gun at his waist. She screamed but the sound was drowned out by the deafening roar of gunfire. In the stunned silence that followed the shot, she barely heard her brother's prolonged, terrified scream.

Blue smoke rose from the gun as if in exaggeratedly slowed motion. A laugh echoed from the shooter. Her father jerked in mid step, took a sudden awkward plunge forward. He hit the floor on his face, on the back of his white shirt a blooming orchid of scarlet.

Tootie screamed again, grabbing her brother's arm.

The tall man suddenly filled the kitchen doorway, his spidery fingers clamped about her mother's arm. Allison del Pelado's face was battered, her hair disheveled, peasant dress torn at the shoulder.

'Christ, you could have at least given me time to get my pecker up,' the tall man said, shaking his head while looking down at the unmoving form of her father.

The man at the window shrugged, then swung his gun at Tootie. 'Shut the hell up, you stupid brat.'

She went quiet and Alejandro gripped her tight, trying to comfort her, though tears streamed from his eyes.

Her father was dead. She was certain of it. And a great searing pain like none she'd ever felt tore through her heart.

'We can't stay here, now,' the tall man said, frowning, his gaunt face looking skeletal. 'They find us here with bodies it's a necktie party and I ain't ready to be the guest of honor. I got a reputation to uphold.'

The other man nodded. 'What about her?' He ducked his chin at Tootie's mother.

The taller man shrugged, then whisked up his gun and jammed it to the woman's temple.

Tootie tried to scream, 'No!' but before the word even left her mouth the man jerked the trigger and sent a bullet into her mother's brain.

Her mother flew sideways out of his grip and slammed into the wall, rebounding and crumpling to the floor in a lifeless heap. Half her head had disappeared with the shot. The tall man frowned, flicking pieces of bone and brain-matter from his frock-coat sleeve.

'Christamighty, I've ruined another coat,' he said, then holstered his gun.

Tears streamed from Tootie's eyes and Alejandro clung to her in a death hug.

The man at the window turned his gun towards them and Tootie saw death in his eyes. 'Can't have no other witnesses, can we?' he said.

'Leave them be,' said the taller man, grinning. 'Reckon if you youngun's don't want us coming back and doing what we did to your parents you'll keep your mouths shut.'

'You can't be serious?' the other man said, shock on his face. 'We can't just leave witnesses.'

The tall man's dark gaze fell upon them and Tootie returned a look of hate.

'They ain't witnesses, they're children. They can't tell the law nothin' 'cept two men came and killed their folks. I want them to recollect this day. It'll show them life ain't worth a damn 'less you take what you want. I want them to see this day in their nightmares till they die.'

An indescribable cruelty filled the man's dark eyes. He was a monster, the Devil himself, in Tootie's mind, and if she could have reached the Winchester she would have filled him full of lead.

'You're one cruel sonofabitch, Jimmy boy, you know that?' the man at the window said with a lilt in his voice. 'Maybe I could have the girl to . . . you know. . . .'

The taller man grinned and moved towards the door. 'You're a sick bastard. Leave her be. We ain't got time to drag along a youngun' for your pleasure.'

The other man shrugged, then followed the tall man out the door. Tootie struggled from her brother's grip and leaped to her feet. Alejandro seemed frozen to the sofa, face streaming tears, teeth clenched until white balls of muscle stood out on either side of his jaw.

She raced to the Winchester, grabbing a hard-backed chair on the way, then propping it beneath the wall rack, which was too high for her to reach. She climbed onto the chair and snatched the rifle from its pegs, surprised at how heavy the weapon was. She almost dropped it, had all she could do to raise it level after she jumped from the chair.

From outside came the sound of hoofbeats, as two horses whirled and headed across the grounds.

She ran to the door, then out onto the porch. She did her best to aim the heavy rifle at the retreating killers.

She pulled the trigger.

A hollow *clack* sounded.

Her father didn't keep the Winchester loaded, she suddenly recollected. The bullets were in a drawer of the desk against the parlor wall. She'd never be able to load it before those men disappeared. They had already reached the edge of the property. Another few seconds would take them from sight.

She dropped the rifle. Sobs shuddered through her body and she began to scream at them, words her parents would likely have thought she didn't know. She screamed and screamed until her throat went raw and sound would no longer come out. Then she collapsed and cried, cried like she had never cried before, cried until no tears remained inside her.

Tootie shot bolt upright in bed, a scream lodged in her throat. Her heart thundered in her ears and tears flooded her eyes. For an instant she remained stunned, gasping, then realized she was in the hotel room, in bed, Jim Hannigan beside her.

'It was only a nightmare. . . .' she told herself, then buried her face in her hands, tears flowing, sobs racking her body. She hadn't dreamt of that day for so very long, hadn't relived the horror of it in years. For countless nights after their murder that horrible day had played itself out in her dreams. Then one day the nightmares had simply vanished, buried themselves deep, where, she reckoned, they'd rot and never plague her again. She had outgrown them, used her strength to subdue them.

But something had dredged the nightmare to the surface again, and she knew what that something was. Now she knew who had killed her parents and the knowledge made her quiver uncontrollably, made her chest feel as if an iron band had cinched around it. Now she knew the man responsible, the monster who had set her life on a course of grief and loneliness. And by some bastard quirk of fate that man lay a charred corpse in a grave at the edge of town.

James Deadwood. Gunslinger. Legend. Murderer. The man with him that day was likely his partner, Edgecomb, or some unknown bandit who'd met his fate elsewhere or was running free, enjoying the spoils of blood.

All these years, she'd searched for a clue to the murderer of Allison and Juan del Pelado, coming up empty. Now she had found the man, and now she could not have the one thing she wanted most – to see him die.

He had been younger, then, much younger, without the mustache, but those eyes, those eyes had not changed. And after Hannigan had shown her the tintype those eyes had drilled into her mind and unearthed the memory she had suppressed for so long. Now she knew why the sight of Deadwood had frozen her. Now she had the answer to her parents' deaths and it came with not only gushing relief but with tremendous disappointment and sorrow, because to have him die by the hand of some anonymous men felt so . . . empty.

'Tootie?' came a voice beside her. She felt his touch on her bare shoulder and drew her face from her hands.

It took a minute to compose herself enough even to speak. 'I'm sorry . . . I didn't mean to wake you. . . .'

He sat up beside her, putting his arm around her shoulders, then brushed a stray lock of hair from her tear-dampened face.

'What happened?' His voice came low and gentle and she felt like blurting out everything, but held it in. If she told him now she would fall apart.

'It's . . . nothing. Just hold me, please.' She placed her face against his chest and he held her tight. A few moments later she stopped shaking and could hear his heart beating instead of the thunder of her own thoughts.

CHAPTER SIX

Hannigan arose early, dressed and left Tootie sleeping in the hotel room. She'd remained awake most of the night, only drifting off near dawn. He didn't have the heart to wake her, so he left a note for her with the clerk, explaining where he'd be going.

He wondered what had caused her such terror. She hadn't stopped shaking for an hour. A nightmare, surely, but of what? Her brother? She would tell him in time, he reckoned, but she didn't wear fear well and he didn't like seeing it on her. It made him feel helpless and that wasn't a feeling he cottoned to.

The early morning carried a chill and the scent of decay. Leaves, whisked by a brisk breeze, skittered across the rutted street. Ice coated puddles and frost glazed windowpanes.

At the café he ate a quick breakfast of eggs, biscuits and coffee. In his mind, he replayed the previous day's events, searching for a connection to the gunfighter's supposed murder. Something about James Deadwood's death bothered him, but he wasn't sure what. Maybe it was the way the marshal and doc had lied; he felt certain both were covering up something. Maybe it was the charred body or lack of blood in the room above the saloon. Maybe it was the bullet pumped into a prone body in that room or the ghost that had appeared on the mezzanine. Whatever the case, his Pinkerton friend had been right to suspect something amiss.

Hannigan leaned back in his café chair, then took a sip of coffee, pondering. Just who was James Deadwood? Killer or savior? Man or monster?

Arrogant, the gunslinger never missed a chance to tell his own exaggerated version of his adventures. In itself that meant little; too many of the West's so-called heroes came cut out of whole cloth and let their pride varnish truth. But was Deadwood more than that? Was he a cold-blooded killer? A man whose legend was built on the graves of the innocent?

He'd wondered about Tootie's peculiar reaction to the man's likeness on the tintype, so before he'd joined her at the saloon last night he'd taken another look at the photo. It probably had been there all the time, caught by the camera, but since he hadn't been looking for it, he'd missed it – a darkness no man could totally disguise. It was in the eyes, he reckoned. Deadwood's eyes were the eyes of a man who likely didn't only stray from the path of righteousness but forged his own trail across the valley of evil. Hannigan should have noticed it when they met, maybe had, but at the time he had been green, perhaps a little star-struck by the man's legend.

A legend that called James Deadwood the fastest gunfighter who ever lived.

Time and experience had tarnished that legend in Hannigan's mind. Deadwood was merely a man to him, now, likely a vicious killer. A man who, if still alive, Hannigan would have to bring in to answer pending charges or face down in a gunfight. And if the latter were even a possibility, he needed something better than the sawed off Peacemaker at his hip. The gun was designed to do more damage at closer range, but he sacrificed a hair's worth of speed, a measure of accuracy.

After finishing his coffee in two gulps, he left the café and sauntered towards a gunshop he'd noticed on his way to the saloon last night. Few townsfolk strolled along the boardwalk; the ones who did ignored him. The town lived at night, existed during the day. Decent folk likely shied away from Autumn Pass, though he noted a couple cowboys entering the mercantile and a woman who looked to be a schoolmarm entering the dress-shop, the second destination on Hannigan's itinerary.

Deadwood reportedly had no kin, no brothers who might resemble him, no wife. Intelligence said nothing about a daughter, either, but that contradicted what Annalea had told Tootie last night. Hannigan aimed to question the girl at the dress-shop and determine the truth.

A bell jangled above the door as he entered the gunshop, summoning a man from the back room. The proprietor scurried out like a little red rabbit. Older than Hannigan, perhaps in his late forties, he sported a thatch of unkempt hair the color of old pumpkin. Freckles plastered his nose and cheeks. He couldn't have topped more than five foot two.

The gunshop man jerked to a stop when his gaze met Hannigan.

Hannigan pushed the door closed, a sliver of a smile creasing his lips. 'Reckon it's been a spell, Red.'

'Christ, Hannigan, I'm a legitimate shop-owner now, I swear. Whoever said I done somethin's talkin' out their backside.'

The man stammered the words and his body acquired a tremble.

Hannigan uttered a chopped laugh, then went to the counter and plucked his Peacemaker from its holster. He shot a glance at some of the weapons displayed about the shop, then peered at Red.

'Relax, I'm not here for you. I'm here for a new gun.' He placed his gun on the counter.

Red stuttered a nod, then scurried to the back of the counter and peered at Hannigan's stunted piece.

'Looks like it's had its share of use,' he murmured.

'Reckon that's an accurate observation. But I need your best, not what you got displayed around your shop. I reckon you know it's in your best interest not to try to pull the wool over my eyes?'

Red jerked another nod, frowned, then disappeared into the back. He returned a moment later with a Peacemaker, which he set on the counter beside Hannigan's piece.

The damn thing nearly glowed, its steel polished to a slick shine, its ivory grip a masterpiece of workmanship. Hannigan hefted the gun then slid it into his holster. In a blurred move he drew the weapon again, bringing it to aim at a spot on the east wall. He slid it back into the holster, withdrew it, sighted down the barrel.

'Christ, I can't hardly even foller your draw,' Red said, shaking a bit harder. 'Ain't never seen nothin' so fast.'

'That a fact?' Hannigan said. 'Not even from James Deadwood?'

The man's face paled, but Hannigan didn't know whether that came from recognition of the man's name or something more immediate. 'Never met the man. . . .'

Hannigan eyed him, cocking a brow. 'You wouldn't lie to me, now, would you, Red?'

'Like I said, Hannigan, I'm legit now. I only run my shop in this town—'

'Because owlhoots buy more guns than decent folk.'

Red shrugged. 'Man's gotta eat.'

'That seems to be the theme in this town. But a man's takin' his chances with that type. Someday your luck might run out and one of 'em won't want to pay for his piece.'

Red's expression told Hannigan the notion had occurred to him but greed had overcome any reservations.

'You sold to Deadwood, by any chance?' Hannigan

asked, sighting down the Peacemaker's barrel again.

'Like I said, never met the man. He's just some-one you read about and pray you don't encounter.' Red reached beneath the counter and pulled up a tattered dime novel. He tossed it beside Hannigan's stunted Peacemaker.

Hannigan glanced at it. '*James Deadwood Rides Again*. Reckon the author put a lot of thought into that title.'

'Hell of a read, though, if you like that sort of thing, I mean. Read some of the ones they writ about you, too.'

Hannigan chuckled, shook his head. 'Don't believe everything you read – I'll take this gun . . . if you give me a fair price.'

It took fifteen minutes of haggling and the exchange of Hannigan's sawed-off for 'souvenir purposes' – Red planned to mount the weapon and proclaim the mighty Jim Hannigan had purchased from him – to reach a deal.

Another fifteen minutes found the manhunter outside the dress-shop.

Hannigan entered the dress-shop, his gaze sweeping across the racks of dresses, tables holding bolts of material and various feminine accessories he had little knowledge off. He wondered if he wouldn't have been better off sending Tootie here to deal with the daughter, and then worried she was going to let him have an earful for doing it without her.

Two women occupied the shop, a younger woman hanging a dress on a rack who looked up as he came in, and an older woman, whom he took to be the owner.

'You don't look like the type who wears a dress,' the older woman said, a slight smile crossing her lips.

'I'm looking for a woman,' he said, closing the door, then stepping deeper into the shop.

'You might want to try the saloon in that case.' The older woman's smile widened. She was heavy-set, wearing a pink flowered dress that did little for her ripe figure. Her hair was yanked back into a sharp bun.

He doffed his hat, gave her a pleasant smile. 'A specific woman, daughter of James Deadwood.'

'I'm Aurella Deadwood,' said the younger woman. She had finished hanging the dress and came around the garments, then up to Hannigan.

'Ma'am.' He tilted his head in greeting. 'Name's Jim Hannigan. I'm here to ask you about your father.'

'He was a bastard.' Genuine spite laced the girl's tone. He studied her, the long brown hair that cascaded over her shoulders, the generous curves of her figure unconcealed by a tight-fitting blue ging-ham, the attractive yet hard lines of her face. Her brown eyes showed a measure of wear, as if her life had been troubled, and he reckoned that with a father like Deadwood that was likely the case. Something about her looked out of place, however. She impressed him as a woman putting on an air, playacting at being innocent, but maybe that related back to having a gunslinger as a father as well.

84

'I hear tell. But I reckon you got a specific reason for saying that?'

Her face darkened and she folded her arms about herself. 'He fornicated with my mom, then left her. She had me and he had his mighty reputation. My mom died a short time after I was born and I got sent to homes, hating him more with every day that passed.'

'So I reckon you didn't come to Autumn Pass to pay your final respects. . . ?'

The woman's eyes narrowed, fury sparking within them. 'I came here to kill him. Only some sonofabitch beat me to it.'

Hannigan nodded. 'Wasn't aware that Deadwood had a daughter, or any kin for that matter.'

'He don't, least not in the real sense of the word. He had a child, a child who hates his very name and every day I'm here I go out and spit on his grave.'

'Why stay, then, in this town? It's a hell-hole.'

She shrugged, features tightening. 'Just who are you, Mr Hannigan? Why are you interested in my no-good father?'

He gazed out through the dress-shop window, debating what he should tell her and deciding he'd be best just to come out with the truth and see where it led. 'I was hired to make sure your father was dead, as reports claimed. I got reason to think he might not be.'

The shock on the girl's face came and went in a heartbeat but he knew his words had startled her. 'You can't be serious? Alive?'

He nodded. ' 'Less you believe in ghosts.'

'Ghosts?'

'He was seen at the saloon last night, least folks think they saw him. I checked out where he had been killed and his corpse and things about both don't add up right in my estimation.'

The girl studied him a moment, her face taking on an almost a cunning expression. 'So you think maybe he faked his death? Why?'

Something in her voice made him wonder about her motives for asking, something that said the idea of Deadwood being still alive appealed to her just fine, and maybe that was because she wanted a chance to put him in the ground herself.

Hannigan shrugged. 'With the indictments he's got pending against him, he stood a good chance of hanging for certain crimes. I figure he wanted to escape that.'

'Man like him is known, though. Someone would see him and tell.'

He nodded. 'Likely, but I might be dead wrong. That man lying in the grave outside of town might really be your father. On the other hand. . . .'

'He may be still walkin' around free. . . .' The girl's tone had grown almost cheerful.

'If you should see him, miss, don't try to take him down yourself, no matter how angry you are at him. Surely you realize he's a dangerous man? He's killed more than fifty men, according to accounts.'

'Reputations are usually overblown, Mr Hannigan.'

'Some have a grain of fact, too. Your father's no one to play with. You see him, you come to the hotel and let me know. I'm staying in room six.'

She gave him a smile that suddenly made her look much less innocent than she put on. 'I'll be sure to do that, Mr Hannigan. I've heard of you, by the way. You got a reputation almost as big as my father's, 'cept I hear you ain't got the same eye for the ladies. . . .'

'Not sure what you're gettin' at, miss, but I reckon one's enough for me.'

'Is it?' She stepped closer to him and he could smell the scent of her perfume, feel the heat from her body.

He backed up, setting his hat on his head as he did so. 'You recollect what I said. Don't try to take him down yourself should he be alive.'

She laughed and he didn't like the mocking tone it carried.

After he left the dress-shop, he wondered just what the hell Deadwood's daughter was thinking and decided he wasn't getting any better at reading a woman's thoughts.

One thing he had concluded from their talk: the girl had not seen Deadwood, or the gunfighter might indeed have been amongst the buried.

With a prickle of frustration, he figured he was running out of options. It occurred to him he might never be able to prove whether Deadwood was really dead or alive unless the man showed himself, or he caught those involved in the death or disappearance. All he had for suspects were the doc and the marshal, both of whom were hiding something, he felt certain, but getting either to talk was problematic. The doc might prove easier to break, but the marshal was the type who might go running to whoever pulled his strings. That someone was pulling them Hannigan had little doubt. The lawdog was too lazy to do much of his own thinking. He'd start there, he decided, with the more difficult of the two.

A few minutes later, Hannigan stepped into the marshal's office. He entered to discover the lawman slumped in the chair behind his desk. The girl from the saloon, Annalea, knelt on the floor at his feet. Hannigan couldn't see what she had been doing beneath the desk but her make-up was smeared when she looked up and a ripening bruise glowed on her face. Her peek-a-boo blouse was torn, leaving little to the imagination.

The lawdog frowned. 'Hannigan, what the hell you doin' here this time of the morning?' The marshal's tone dripped irritation. His hands dropped below desk-level, likely buttoning his trousers, Hannigan figured. The girl cast the manhunter a plaintive look and with the back of her hand wiped a dribble of blood from her mouth.

'Startin' a mite early, aren't you, Hooper?' Hannigan frowned, glancing again at the girl, who averted her gaze.

'Jesus H, there's a specific time for gettin' your bell rung, now? No one told me.' The marshal leaned forward, then plucked a bill from his shirt pocket and tossed it at the girl. She took it, stuffing it in her skirt as she slowly came to her feet. She cast

Hannigan a sad look, then scooted past him and left the office.

Hannigan eyed the marshal after she had left. 'She's a mite young, don't you think?'

'Younger the better, I figure. Old enough to bleed, as the sayin' goes.'

Hannigan shook his head. 'You're a disgusting pig, Hooper. Make no mistake about it, I don't like you and I'm never going to.'

Hooper cocked an eyebrow. 'Well, hell, there goes the deputy job I was plannin' on offerin' you.'

'I want some answers and I'm not leaving your dirty little hole of a town 'til I get them.'

Crimson bled into the lawdog's cheeks. 'I gave you your goddamn answers yesterday. Get the hell out of my town.'

'Care to personally try throwing me out? Maybe you want to arrange my death like Deadwood's?'

'What the goddamn hell are you talkin' about, Hannigan? The killin' you done driven you plum loco?'

He ignored the remark. 'I dug up Deadwood's grave, Hooper. That was no Apache cremation and like I told my partner, Apaches bury their dead in crevices. I figure someone burned that body to hide something. I ain't so sure that person might not be you.'

'Prove it.' The fire in the marshal's tone had receded just a hair, telling Hannigan he might have struck a nerve.

'Damned if I don't aim to. Took a look at where Deadwood was killed, too. Not enough blood in the room.' Hannigan reached into his shirt pocket, brought out the slug he'd pried from the floor, then dropped it onto the marshal's desk. 'This was in the floor. Someone shot a body already lying there by the looks of it. That combined with too little blood tells me whoever got shot in that room was already dead before that bullet hit him.'

'You're loco, awright. Get the hell out of my office!'

The marshal appeared a little more rattled now; Hannigan heard it in his voice, saw it in a slight twitching of his cheek. He smiled to himself. The lawdog's reaction convinced him all the more that something untoward was going on in this town.

'Watch yourself, Marshal.' Hannigan moved towards the door. 'I find out you've got your hand in anything related to Deadwood and I'll be back. And I won't be so cordial next time.'

Hannigan stepped out of the office and closed the door. He heard a *thunk* from inside and reckoned the lawdog had hurled something against a wall in frustration. For the first time that morning Hannigan felt a measure of satisfaction.

Marshal Hooper waited a good two hours after Hannigan left before getting out of his chair and crossing the room to the door. Fact was, despite his bravado, the manhunter scared the living hell out of him almost as much as Deadwood and he had pissed his britches right before Hannigan left. His trousers were still wet but fear had gotten the better of him and he needed to make arrangements about that sonofabitch before he got any closer to the truth.

Hooper stepped out into the daylight, peering in every direction to make certain Hannigan was nowhere to be seen. He waddled his way to the saloon, puffing heavily by the time he got there.

The place was empty, except for the 'keep, who nodded to him. Hooper went up the stairs, feeling a spike of pain stab his chest. He worried again that he would die right then and there.

But he didn't and by the time he stepped into the darkened room four the pain had subsided enough to tell him he was going to live another day.

He banged on the wall, then went to the bed and waited. A moment later someone stood in the room with him, bathed in shadow.

'Goddammit, this is getting to be a powerful bad habit,' came a whispered voice laced with irritation.

Hooper grunted. 'Can't be helped. Hannigan came to visit me again. He dug up the body and figured out what happened in this room. That little appearance last night didn't help matters none, either.'

No sound came from the other for a moment. 'I'll take care of it.'

'Soon? He ain't gonna let up.'

'Soon.'

CHAPTER SEVEN

Jim Hannigan entered the café a little after eleven o'clock. He'd gone back to the hotel only to find that Tootie had woken and left word with the manager that she'd be at the eatery.

Most of the half-dozen tables covered with blue-checked cloth were empty and the scents of coffee and beefsteak filled the air.

He spotted Tootie sitting at the rear table, a cup in her hand, her gaze focused on some spot beyond the window. Her expression appeared melancholy.

He made his way to the table, doffed his hat and tossed it onto a seat next to the one he sat in. Tootie looked over at him and gave him a thin smile.

Hannigan signaled the waitress to bring another cup. The girl set it before him a moment later. He poured himself a cup of Arbuckle's and waited for Tootie to break the silence.

'Get anything out of her?' Tootie asked, voice low.

Hannigan shook his head. 'Nothing particularly useful. Your bargirl was right, though, Aurella Deadwood looks out of place in that dress-shop.

Might just be because she's the daughter of a gunslinger, whom she despises, incidentally, or might be she isn't who she claims to be. One thing for sure, she was damn near elated when I told her Deadwood might still be alive because she's got a notion to stop his clock on her own.'

Tootie nodded, face darkening. She had dressed in her riding-skirt and tan blouse and her hair hung loose about her face. Dark half-circles nested under her eyes and Hannigan could see the remnants of the previous night's terror in her eyes.

'I reckon I'll visit her myself after we're done here. Won't tell her I'm workin' with you. I'll pretend to be lookin' for a new dress. Women are better at judging other women. Men let their better judgement go down the crick when they see a pretty face.'

He uttered a chopped laugh. 'How do you know she's pretty?'

She raised an eyebrow. 'Isn't she?'

He shrugged. 'If you go for that type. I didn't know you better, Miss del Pelado, I'd say you were a mite jealous.'

'Then you don't know me well enough, Mr Hannigan. We'll have to rectify that.'

He smiled, gazed out into the street, silent a moment, then looked back to Tootie. 'Was going to wait for you to pick your time to tell me but I reckon I don't like the pain I'm seein' in your eyes. What's wrong, Tootie?'

She looked at the table, with a fingertip absently tracing the rim of her cup. Looking back up to him, she frowned. 'I had a nightmare . . . of the day my parents were killed. I haven't dreamt of that day in years. I had tucked it away, figuring that after spending so much time looking for their killers and coming up empty there was no chance of finding them.'

'Something happen to jolt the memory?' He took a sip of his coffee and waited for her to collect her thoughts. He saw tears shimmer in her eyes, unspilled.

'I know who killed them, now. I couldn't recollect either man's face . . . until you showed me that tintype of Deadwood.'

Something sank in his belly and his gaze locked with hers. 'Deadwood—'

'Murdered my mother.' Her lips quivered and her eyelids fluttered. 'There was a second man with him, a shorter, skinny man who followed his orders. He shot my father. Maybe it was his partner, Edgecomb, or maybe it was somebody else who rode with him. Deadwood never addressed him by name.'

'You're sure? Sometimes memory plays tricks.'

She shook her head. 'I'm sure. He didn't have the mustache then, was younger, but those eyes of his . . . He left me and Alejandro alive to suffer. Didn't even have the decency to kill us and save us a lifetime of grief.'

'Doesn't matter for what reason he left you alive. All that matters is that he did and you're doing your damnedest to make the lives of others better because of it. Won't bring back your loved ones, but your life has meanin' and I'm the luckiest man alive for having you with me.'

'Why, Jim Hannigan, I do declare, that might just be the least awkward thing you ever said to me.' She offered a weak smile, some of the light coming back into her eyes.

He felt his cheeks heat. 'Just don't expect it too often. I ain't a man who's good with words.' He smiled back.

Tootie's gaze drifted back out through the window. 'If he's dead I'll never have the chance to make him pay for what he did. I wanted to kill him myself.'

'Reckon there's a lot of that going around where he's concerned.' He took another sip of his coffee. He saw a tear slip down her cheek, which she quickly brushed away.

'Don't know how much more pain I can take. First Alejandro . . .' She swallowed hard, sniffled. 'I thought I was strong, but I feel . . . I feel like that little girl again, watching those men take away everything that had meanin' in my life, watchin' them destroy my childhood.'

He placed his hand over hers. She gripped it, her lips quivering harder.

'If Deadwood's alive we'll make him pay. If he's not, he got what he deserved, even if you didn't give it to him.'

'There's still another man out there somewhere. . . .'

'If it's Edgecomb, we'll track him down. I'll have my Pinkerton friend locate a photo of him. He might have changed a lot in thirteen years.'

'Even after my dream I can hardly see his face. It was nondescript, not like Deadwood's. Doubt I'd know him if I saw him again 'less he looked exactly the way he did then.'

He nodded and they remained silent for long moments. He wished he could comfort her more, but the nightmare had reopened old wounds and she would need time for them to heal.

'Had a parley with the marshal after I visited Deadwood's daughter. Rattled his cage, I reckon. Maybe it'll lead somewhere if he has any involvement in this case. Watched his office for an hour or so but he didn't come out. That bargirl was with him when I got there, incidentally. She looked worse for wear.'

'I wish I could help her, but—'

'You did what you could. Rest is up to her. From the look in her eyes she'll either kill him sooner or later or leave this town.'

'Where she'll find another fella just like him and just repeat the story 'til someone buries her.'

'You can't change the whole world, Tootie. Folks will choose their own paths and be who they want to be. You do the best you can to save those who want to be saved. That's the most you can ask of yourself.'

She peered at him. 'I just want to change one, Jim. I just want to take one little girl out of this hole and set her on a straight path. I could have been her. . . .'

'But you're not. You're strong. You held on to your humanity. That's more than too many in these parts can lay claim to, even under the best of life's circumstances.'

'The world's going to hell, isn't it?'

'Some say it's always been hell, just the times change. Reckon I see it different. Reckon no matter how much filth I run across there's always hope. The decent folk in this world make everything worthwhile.'

She gave him a soft laugh. 'Jim Hannigan, the philosopher. Who'd ever have thought it?'

'Don't spread it around.' He grinned. 'You up for getting some food in you?'

'Reckon I could use a bit now.' She smiled a warm smile. 'And thank you. . . .'

'For what?'

'For everything.' She lifted his hand and pressed her lips to it. A warm sensation trickled through him. Maybe he was getting used to this emotion thing after all.

After Tootie finished a late breakfast, Hannigan headed back to the hotel for a shave while she went to the dress-shop to question Aurella Deadwood.

When he reached the top of the stairs, he stopped, noticing a woman standing in the hall outside his door. He frowned, then approached her.

'Miss Deadwood. . . ?' he said, as he reached her.

She smiled, a smile that was probably supposed to be innocent but came with a sultry edge.

'Mr Hannigan. I thought over what you said about my father. I wanted to talk to you about him. Mind if I come in?' She was wearing a different dress, this one tighter, its saffron material stretched taut across her bosom, which she accentuated by pulling back her shoulders.

The notion of inviting her into his room suddenly gave him a pang of discomfort, which probably had everything to do with the thought of a certain fiery partner discovering he'd let a woman other than herself into his hotel room.

He nodded, then plucked the key from his pocket and unlocked the door. The girl followed him into the room. She left the door ajar and he felt only marginally relieved.

'What's on your mind, Miss Deadwood?' he asked, folding his arms.

She took a step closer to him and he got a whiff of her flowery perfume again; it was damn near intoxicating.

'I thought over what you said, about him being dangerous and me not trying to take him down alone. I want you to find him. I hear tell you dispense vengeance. I want you to dispense it for me. I want to hire you.'

He almost laughed but wasn't sure how sincere the girl was. 'You likely couldn't afford me, Miss Deadwood.'

'Aurella, please. . . .'

'Aurella. But I'm already looking for him, if he is indeed alive and that's still in doubt. And assuming I do find him alive you'd likely have to wait your turn in line putting a bullet in him. Appears someone else has more at stake in the matter than you.'

'Who?' She took another step closer, stopping

mere inches from him. He suppressed the urge to step back.

'That doesn't matter for now. I'll do my best to find out the truth. I'll see to it you learn it, too. That's the most I can offer.'

'Is it?' Her face darkened a little and her lips worked a pout. He got the distinct impression she was playacting again and not doing a particularly subtle job at it. She suddenly stepped up against him and pressed her lips to his. Her kiss was cold, hard, and he immediately pulled away. She threw her arms around his neck and clung to him. He struggled to dislodge her as she tried to kiss him again.

'I can be real nice to you, Mr Hannigan,' she said. 'You help me find my father and I'll give you anything you want from me. I know how to please a man.'

He frowned and broke her hold, pushed her back. 'This ain't proper, Miss Deadwood.'

'The hell with propriety. You're a fella and you got needs. I can satisfy them.'

His voice went cold. 'I reckon you're used to getting what you want with your body, miss. Maybe that would have worked with me in the past but what I got now's too important to risk and far better than anything you could offer.'

Anger flashed in her eyes. She wasn't used to being turned down, that was plain. 'You got no idea what you're passing up, Hannigan.'

'And what exactly *would* that be?' came a voice from the door. Hannigan looked over to see Tootie standing against the jamb, her palm flat against the door she had just pushed inwards. He wondered just how much she had overseen and overheard and felt his belly sink.

Aurella turned, looking Tootie up and down. 'Who the hell are you?'

'Name's Tootie and I'd tell you why men think I got that name, but I reckon you'd be versed in such things already.'

The anger in Aurella Deadwood's eyes strengthened. 'You a whore?'

Tootie's eyes narrowed. 'Might ask you the same question.'

Aurella looked back to Hannigan, who stood as rigid as a man holding sweating dynamite. 'She your woman?'

'Yes, Mr Hannigan,' Tootie said, cocking an eyebrow. 'Do tell, am I your woman?' A nasty little smirk followed the question, which he didn't appreciate a hell of a lot.

'She's my woman,' he answered without hesitation, knowing what was good for him.

Aurella glanced back at Tootie, shaking her head. 'Don't look like much. Looks like one night might break her.'

'Reckon you best take your leave, Miss Deadwood,' he said.

Aurella made a disgusted sound and uttered a phrase Hannigan had only heard come out of drovers and outlaws, which referred to an act she was likely well practiced in. She spun on her shoe-toe and cast Tootie a spiteful glance as she strode past her into the hall. Tootie watched from the door and Hannigan heard the girl's footsteps recede.

'Am I in trouble?' he asked, hoping the other shoe wasn't about to drop.

Tootie laughed, then stepped into the room. She closed the door, came over to him and kissed him deeply. Pulling away, she smiled. 'That better than what she gave you?'

'I take it that means you were standing there a spell?'

'Long enough to see her jump your rangy bones and try to swallow your tongue.'

'In my defense I did nothing to encourage her.'

Tootie laughed. 'Also long enough to hear you tell her you wouldn't risk what you had.'

'But you enjoyed making me squirm?'

'It uplifted my mood.'

'Glad I could provide you some entertainment.'

'Don't let it happen again.' Tootie pulled away and went to the bed, sat on the edge. She leaned back, both palms pressed to the mattress. 'So what did she want? I went to the shop and the owner told me she had gone out for a spell but she didn't know where. I came back here to find you entertaining.'

'She wanted to hire me, she said, and apparently figured she could offer her services in lieu of payment.'

'Bet it ain't the first time she's done that. She might be Deadwood's daughter but I don't see any resemblance and it's a safe bet she's worked her ass before.'

He nodded. 'I got the notion she's got something

else on her mind besides simple revenge on her father.'

'You, from the looks of it.' She chuckled.

'Besides me. She's up to something.'

'Long as you ain't.' She grinned and he knew she was getting way too much enjoyment out of his discomfort.

'It was like kissing a catfish.'

'I like that answer.'

He smiled. 'Hoped you would.'

'I'm going to pay her another visit, right about the time the shop closes. Now that she knows who I am I reckon I can go straight at her.'

'Best be careful. If she's Deadwood's daughter she might be more dangerous than she looks.'

'Hell hath no fury like a woman catching another trying to steal her man. She best watch out for *me*.'

Hannigan almost pitied Aurella Deadwood then.

Marshal Hooper leaned against a supporting beam in front of his office, gaze drifting towards the hotel. He felt like waltzing right on over there and putting a goddamn bullet between Hannigan's eyes for making a fool of him earlier, but he knew it was a piss-poor idea if he had a notion to go on living. He'd have to be content with letting others deal with the manhunter.

A woman leaving the hotel broke his reverie. He watched her step off the boardwalk and cross the street. She strode towards the dress-shop with a stiffness of carriage and determination of gait that told him she was angered over something.

Something in the pit of his belly twisted with his recognition of the woman and the realization that she must have contacted the manhunter. Jesus H, that was just what they needed, her conspiring with Hannigan. Bad enough she'd ridden in here claiming to be Deadwood's daughter and then stayed for some reason known only to herself. What the hell was she up to now?

Things were starting to fall apart, Hooper thought. In all their years running this operation nothing like this had even come close to happening. Now the town was crawling with potential hazards, any one of them enough to ruin their plans and get them all strung up.

He sighed. Hannigan wasn't the only one something needed to be done about: the so-called Miss Aurella Deadwood had just moved up the list.

CHAPTER EIGHT

Nightfall came early now in Autumn Pass. The distant mountains seemed to gobble the sun and make the town even more goddamn depressing than it was already, far as Aurella Deadwood saw it. She was sick to death of this god-forsaken hole and she'd only been here a short while. She was sick to death of working in this goddamn dress-shop, too, pretending to be someone she was not. How did women tolerate such nonsense when a gal could make a hell of a lot more cash lying on her back?

She gazed out through the shop window at the darkened street, lips drawn tight. She hated this town, this shop and the pathetic old woman who owned it. She hated Jim Hannigan for having the goddamn nerve to turn down her advances and that woman she reckoned was his. What did that no-good mattress-warmer have that she didn't? That tramp might as well have been a boy for all the tit the Good Lord had seen fit to provide her. She was nowhere near the woman Aurella was, probably couldn't satisfy a man any better than one of those sexless nuns she'd heard tell of.

'Pfft!' She spat at the wooden floor and wrapped her arms about herself. Most of all she hated James Deadwood. If that sonofabitch thought he could just run off after makin' her fancy promises, then get his useless hide filled with lead, he had another think comin'. She would get all she had coming to her, that was for damn sure, and more. She hadn't worked him over that well only to be left out in the cold. She recollected the night she had gotten him so plied he'd told her about the years' worth of gold, jewels and cash he'd hidden away somewhere in this town. She aimed to get her fair share of the swag. She deserved it for letting that sonofabitch put his pecker in her.

She shivered, the thought of his calloused hands and greasy mouth bringing bile to her throat. She didn't mind whoring, in fact she liked the power it gave her over men, but that halfbreed ... something about him made her sick inside.

And now the bastard might even be alive, if Hannigan was to be believed. One thing was for sure, she had to beat that manhunter to finding Deadwood and his hideaway or there'd be nothin' left for her. That option would have been a hell of a lot easier had he fallen for her play earlier, but maybe all wasn't lost. That gal couldn't be with him every minute and all men thought with their peckers when the cat was away. And she reckoned no man could resist her for long. A tighter dress, a bit more flesh showing, moist lips and whispered promises ... she'd get to him, even if it meant killing that Tootie woman.

A slight sound brought her from her thoughts. A strange coldness trickled through her. Maybe it was all that talk of ghosts that had been going around today, something about Deadwood's spook appearing in the saloon last night. She reckoned she didn't believe in such nonsense, but standing alone in the darkened shop, shadows bunching in corners and shifting across the floor, made her feel something she rarely experienced: unease, maybe even fear.

'Anyone there?' Her voice sounded unnaturally loud in the stillness of the shop.

Beyond the window the breeze whistled as it slid along the storefront and the autumn chill in the air had already fogged the panes. Barely any light bled in from hanging lanterns in the street.

Jess. . . .

She started, a small sound of fear escaping her lips. It was little more than a harsh whisper, but it seemed to come from everywhere in the room. And a name, one she had not used since coming to this town.

'I'm not Jess!' She spun, trying to peer into each darkened corner. Dresses hanging on racks looked eerily like charred figures without heads; the thought unnerved her all the more. 'I'm Aurella Deadwood.'

A grating laugh shuddered out; her heart stepped up a beat.

'Who's there? Who the hell are you? How'd you get in here?'

Shouldn't have left the back door unlocked, Jess. . . .

'Nobody knows me by that name. . . .' A chilling

thought washed through her mind. *He* did. James Deadwood knew her by that name. Jess Carter, hurdy-gurdy girl from up Montana way. A dollar a dance, two for romance, she told every fella eager to sample her wares. James Deadwood had sampled them voraciously and had continued sampling until the day he ran off on her two weeks ago.

The laugh sounded again, rising in volume. A scrape, like a boot across the floorboards. Something shadowy moved near the back.

She glanced at the front door. She had just locked it, and debated her chances of getting to it and out into the street before he was upon her. She had wanted to find him, it occurred to her, but under *her* terms, not his. That he was here meant he had discovered what she'd come for and had decided to put a stop to it.

Making up her mind to run for the door, she shot one last look behind her. A flash of darkness and something black descended upon her like the Devil's carrion. Hands grabbed her throat, spidery fingers gouging into her soft flesh, crushing her windpipe. Her efforts to break his hold and kick at his legs resulted only in his squeezing harder. Pain splintered through her neck and face; she couldn't even gasp a breath. Weakness flooded her legs and arms.

'Should have left well enough alone, Jess,' the figure said. Her vision blurred. All she could see was a shadowy shape, tall, poised over her, but Deadwood's vile face burned in her mind. 'You should have stayed in Montana and never come here. Was your greed worth your petty little life?'

Her lungs ached, felt as if they were going to burst. The remainder of her strength vanished. She hung in his grip, black rainfall trickling across her mind, then becoming a torrent.

A moment later all pain vanished and she swore she felt the fires of Hell licking at her feet.

With the dusk, Jim Hannigan and Tootie del Pelado came down the hotel stairs. Tootie had told him she planned to go to the dress-shop and see what she could force out of Aurella Deadwood. Hannigan had asked around and discovered that the young woman was staying at the shop at night until she earned enough money to rent a room.

He planned to question the barkeep and perhaps a few of the regulars about last night's 'ghostly visitation'. In a town like this someone might have seen something, though getting them to talk about it was another matter.

'Mr Hannigan?' the manager called to him as he and Tootie reached the bottom of the stairs. The manhunter glanced at the clerk, who was holding out a slip of paper. 'This came for you.'

Hannigan went to the desk. He gave the clerk two bits, then took the note.

'You see who left it?' Hannigan asked.

The manager shook his head. 'Found it here a half-hour ago. Musta come while I was out gettin' my supper.'

Hannigan opened it and glanced at the contents.

'What's it say?' Tootie asked when he returned to her.

'Seems the doc got an attack of conscience. Wants to talk to me. Says he has information about Deadwood.'

'Something smells. . . .' Tootie's brow cinched.

'Like cowflop, but with damn few leads I've got a duty to check it out. Note says to meet him at seven; that gives me fifteen minutes to get there and check out the area before going in.'

She frowned. 'Watch your back. I'm not ready to lose anyone else.'

'Might say the same in your case.' He gave her a gentle smile.

Once out of the hotel Hannigan headed for the doc's and Tootie went towards the dress-shop. The cool night air bit into his face and his boots echoed hollowly on the boardwalk. He heard the jangle of piano music and rowdy cheers echoing from the saloon. The frosty moon glazed the streets with alabaster and brought to mind the notion that ghosts might just haunt a place like Autumn Pass; certainly enough men had died violently in this town to leave their restless spirits behind, if a man believed in such. But Hannigan reckoned any ghost of James Deadwood was likely made of flesh and blood.

As he neared the doc's corner office, he slowed, gaze alert, scanning the area for places where an ambusher might hide. A few cowboys headed towards the Wild Bull, but none gave him a second look. With the nights growing cold most rowdy activity was confined to the saloon. He relaxed, allowing his instincts free rein. Fingers loose, he readied to go for his Peacemaker at the slightest hint of a threat. Something about the doc's note rang false but if a trap meant a lead to Deadwood he had to take the chance.

He paused before the office, peering into the side street that ran along its front. The street appeared deserted, but shadowed alleys branched off, allowing too many places for a bushwhacker to hide.

His hand drifted to the grip of his Peacemaker as he approached the sawbones's door. A light burned within the office, its buttery glow bleeding through a window and spilling across the stoop. He gave the narrow side street another look over, then knocked on the door.

Tootie didn't like the idea that Jim Hannigan might be walking into a trap one bit. She considered turning around and going after him, confronting Aurella Deadwood another time. But if she gave in to her worries and chased after him she'd be doing the same thing she had scolded him for in the past. He was a skilled manhunter, trail-forged and, now that certain matters between them had been brought into the open, a lot more cautious and alert than on their initial cases together.

That didn't stop her from worrying and it would-n't stop her from making this confrontation with Aurella quick – and perhaps even painful for the woman, whom Tootie felt sure was little more than a common bar-tramp – then scooting over to the doc's to cover his back. If he didn't like it, well, that was just too bad.

She uttered a short laugh as she stopped in front of the dress shop. It was the first easy emotion she'd felt since leaving the café with Hannigan. Images from her nightmare and the sight of Deadwood's dark eyes had invaded her thoughts and made her acutely miss her parents for most of the day. The sadness had grown almost unbearable at times, laced with waves of horror as she relived their deaths in her mind. Rage would follow, a fury she hadn't experienced since those early years after the murders. That rage would be with her until she knew whether it was Deadwood lying in that grave, and whether his partner, Edgecomb, had been the second killer there that day. If he were that second man, she would turn over every stone in the West until she found and killed him.

She suppressed the anger surging into her veins and focused on the task ahead. It would do no good to dwell on the past right now, because she had a job to do and she needed to be clear-headed.

The interior of the shop was dark, the place locked up for the night. She banged a fist against the door, guessing Aurella was in there somewhere in the back.

She waited, but heard no sounds from within.

'I know you're in there!' she yelled, then banged again. A moment dragged by. Still no sound.

She glanced behind her, making sure the street was empty. An occasional cowboy went into the saloon, but no one gave her even a passing look.

She knelt, pretending to retie one of the laces on her high-topped shoes. A crimped metal wire ran along the outer edge of the eyelets on either shoe, an apparent ornamentation. As she glanced up and surveyed the street, she pried at the metal piece until it snapped loose. She palmed it, then stood. Hannigan had wondered how she managed to get into locked rooms so easily; if he could see her now, he would know. She inserted the crimped metal piece in the lock, working it for the better part of two minutes until she heard the click she wanted. She knelt again, snapped the metal piece back into place and smiled.

She stood, twisted the knob, then eased the door open. Once in the shop she paused to see if she'd been overheard, but no sound came. She shut the door, then moved deeper into the shop.

'Aurella?' she called, not wanting to startle the girl completely if she were here, and get herself shot. 'Aurella, it's Tootie. I met you at the hotel earlier today. I just wanted to talk to you.' And maybe beat the hell out of you for daring to make a move on my man, she added in her mind, fist clenching.

Her toe hit something. Something soft and yielding. A sudden chill slithering down her spine told her exactly what it was.

She knelt, lips tight, gaze riveting to the dark form of the young woman sprawled at her feet. Her fingers went to the girl's wrist. No pulse, but the body was still warm. She hadn't been dead long.

112

'Oh, damn. . . .' she whispered, then glanced up, wondering if the killer were still in the store.

She came up slowly, hand going to a pocket of her riding-skirt and gripping the derringer within. If the killer had lingered in the shop he'd be sporting two new holes, she reckoned.

It took her only a few minutes of cautious searching to determine that the shop was empty of anyone living. The young woman's killer had fled.

Regret for the young woman pricked her. She wondered just what Aurella had known that had cost her her life. . . .

'What the hell do *you* want?' Doc Butler asked after opening the door. He appeared unsteady, swaying, and gripped the jamb with one hand, the edge of the door with the other. Hannigan wasted no time on courtesies. He shoved past the man into the office, then dug the note from his pocket.

'You tell me, Doc.' He flipped open the note. 'After all, you sent this, didn't you?'

Butler peered at the note, as if having difficulty reading it. 'Me? No, I sent you no note.'

Hannigan had expected as much. 'Says you have information about Deadwood and wanted to talk.'

The words sobered up Butler; his face washed white. Hannigan reckoned that if this were some sort of set-up whoever arranged it had neglected to inform the doctor.

'I sure as hell did *not* send you that note. I already told you everything I knew about Deadwood. Got nothin' more to add.'

'That so?' Hannigan pocketed the note, his nerves singing with irritation. 'From what I can see I haven't gotten a straight answer from anyone in this town since I rode in. I've got me a charred body that might or might not be Deadwood's. I've got damn little blood in the room Deadwood was killed in and a "ghost" haunting the saloon. So forgive me if I don't take your word for it that you've been up front with me.'

An arrogant light flared in the doc's eyes. 'Take it up with Hooper, then. I've got better things to do than entertain the delusions of a has-been manhunter.'

Frustration overwhelming him, Hannigan grabbed two handfuls of Butler's shirt and jammed him against the wall. 'You know, Doc, I never was a very patient sort and the older I get the more I find I haven't improved in that direction. You know anything about Deadwood you best think real hard on telling me, because you don't want me back here on a wild-goose chase again.'

Hannigan released the doctor, then headed for the door. Butler glared at him.

'The marshal will hear about this,' Butler said, face crimson.

'Be downright shocked if he didn't,' Hannigan said, pausing at the door. 'You best hope you had no involvement in Deadwood's murder or disappearance. 'Cause if you did . . . well, plenty of sturdy trees 'bout these parts. . . .'

Hannigan stepped outside, flung the door shut behind him. He felt more certain than ever Butler was involved in something with Hooper, but if he hadn't sent the note, who had and why? He had expected any trap to be sprung before he entered the doc's.

'You were always fast, Hannigan, but never fast enough to beat me. . . .'

The voice startled him more than he cared to admit. A laugh followed, echoing throughout the side street, harsh, grating, a whisper of a thing.

A chill skittered down his spine. He spun towards its source. A dark figure stood at the opposite end of the street, bathed in shadow. The man was tall, slender, wearing a battered hat that shaded his features. A gust ruffled the figure's frock-coat.

The figure simply poised there, hands clasped across his belly, as if waiting.

Shaking off his surprise, Hannigan leaped towards the apparition with far less caution than he should have shown under the circumstances. The sight of the man who could quite possibly be James Deadwood had unnerved him, made him too intent on capturing the gunslinger.

The figure suddenly stepped sideways around a corner at the end of the street. Shadows grew thicker, swallowing. Hannigan angled close to the wall, drawing his Peacemaker, bringing it up near his face.

His shin hit something, something thin and taut but strong. Unable to stop his onward momentum, he pitched forward. He landed hard, breath bursting from his lungs, one hand jamming against the ground, along with his face. The Peacemaker flew from his grip, landing in the dirt a few feet away.

'Christ,' he muttered, pushing himself back up to hands and knees and cursing himself for being careless. He got to his feet, a bit unsteady, hoping to give chase, but it was too late. A narrow back street cut across the one he was on, but he glimpsed no sign of the figure. He listened, heard nothing. He sighed. In the darkness he had virtually no chance of tracking the man.

With a silent curse he knelt, felt about the ground, seeking to discover just what he had tripped over. It took only a moment to locate a length of rawhide string now lying in the dirt. Someone had stretched it from one corner of a wall across the street to a hitch post. Someone who wanted to take no chances when it came to being followed. But what was the point of the appearance? A taunt? That would certainly be like the Deadwood Hannigan recollected, but his manhunter's sixth sense told him there had to be more to it. Deadwood wouldn't risk prolonging Hannigan's stay in town by appearing unless he felt certain the manhunter would no longer pose a threat.

Hannigan stood, annoyed with himself, frustrated with the situation. He located his Peacemaker, shoved the weapon into its holster and turned to walk back down the side street.

An instant later he jerked sideways, catching just the merest glimpse of something flashing towards him in the darkness.

That something hit him a hard, glancing blow. In his distraction over the 'ghost' he had not heard anyone sneaking up on him. With a sudden jarring revelation he realized that that had been the figure's plan all along. Deadwood or whoever was behind this no longer cared whether Hannigan left Autumn Pass – he wanted him to die here.

He should have seen it. That he hadn't sent a bolt of anger through him. There were times he hated to admit he only a human being, not the infallible manhunter the dime novels made him out to be. Because it only took one of those times to get a man killed in his profession and this damn well might prove one of them.

He hit the ground, head throbbing and the world a cyclone of black. He rolled onto his back, gazed up into the spinning darkness. He blinked, and the world settled to a pulsating stop. Two figures stood above him, one of them holding a length of board. Hannigan counted his blessings: the board hadn't caved in his skull completely.

'Goddamn, this was easier'n you would have thunk it, Beckett,' the man clutching the board said.

'Don't get full of yourself, Trigg,' said the second man, who was the taller of the two. 'He weren't distracted you wouldn'ta got that close.'

'The hell I wouldn't!' Trigg said, and sent a kick into Hannigan's face. 'He's all reputation and no balls.'

Hannigan rolled backward, hitting the wall of a building. Pain lanced his face and radiated through his teeth. The gunmetal taste of blood filled his mouth.

Another kick landed, this one against a shoulder. His left arm went momentarily numb.

'Juss finish it, goddammit,' the taller man said. ' 'Fore he gets to his piece.'

Trigg chuckled and lifted his board for another blow. 'Hell, Beckett, just want me a little fun out of killing a famous manhunter first.'

Neither man realized that someone was behind them until the one called Beckett got a tap on his shoulder.

He started, spun. A fist ricocheted from his temple. Beckett stared stupidly for a moment, then crumpled to the dirt, groaning. He struggled to push himself up to hands and knees but had little success.

Trigg burst out laughing. 'Haw-haw-haw, you got yourself felled by an itty bitty girl – erk!'

Tootie grinned and pulled her sharp-toed shoe out of Trigg's crotch. He dropped the board, collapsed, then grabbed his southern parts. He let out a sound like a cat getting skinned.

She backed up a step, dropped something round and dark to the ground, then pulled the derringer from her pocket.

She kept the gun aimed on the men as, a few moments later, they shakily reached their feet.

'We're going to the marshal,' she said. 'And if that man you attacked is hurt bad I'll see to it personally you get fitted for a coffin.'

Trigg glared at her. 'You ain't 'spectin' us to be scart of an itty bitty peashooter like that, are ya?'

'How 'bout one like this?' came Hannigan's

118

voice, followed by the *skritch* of hammer drawing back.

Both men froze, fear crimping their faces. Hannigan stood behind them, Peacemaker leveled on Trigg. He kicked the board out of the way.

'Get going,' he said. 'And keep your hands up.'

Tootie stepped aside as the men filtered out onto the main street.

'How'd you floor that guy with one punch?' Hannigan asked Tootie under his breath.

She smiled. 'I had a rock in my hand.'

Hannigan and Tootie herded the men down the street to the marshal's office. A light burned inside, indicating the lawman hadn't left for the night.

After Tootie opened the door, Hannigan gestured with the Peacemaker for the men to enter.

The marshal, sitting behind the desk, looked up from a dime novel he'd been reading. 'What the Christ?'

'These men attacked me outside the doc's, Marshal. Throw them in a cell.' Hannigan surveyed the men. Neither was much to speak of, common hardcases for hire most likely. The one named Trigg looked a bit more unwashed than his companion and was missing a number of teeth. The one named Beckett was lanky, with a face like old rope.

'Now why the hell should I do that?' The marshal hoisted himself out of his chair and tossed his book to the desk top. 'Just your word against theirs.'

'*Ours,*' Tootie said.

'You're a gal,' the marshal said. 'Your side of the story don't count.' Tootie's face went red.

119

Hannigan's features cinched. 'Lock them up, Hooper, or I swear to God I'll have the county marshal down first thing tomorrow to take a real close look at your little hellhole.'

The marshal glared, but grabbed a set of keys from a wall peg, went to a cell door, then unlocked it. Tootie kept her derringer trained on the two and Hannigan's Peacemaker didn't waver.

'You reckon you want to take their guns, Marshal?' Hannigan asked as the lawdog motioned the men into the cell.

'Huh?' Hooper glanced at the Smith & Wessons strapped to each man's hip. 'Oh, yeah.' He lifted the guns from their holsters, then closed the cell door after they stepped inside.

The marshal returned to his desk, deposited the weapons in a drawer. After tossing the keys onto the blotter, he flopped back into his chair.

He gazed at Hannigan, annoyance in his small eyes. 'Satisfied? You're lucky they didn't just shoot ya.'

'Reckon they wanted it to look like a robbery, though in this town it wouldn't likely matter much.'

'Don't say?' The marshal gave him a smug smile.

'Aurella Deadwood's been murdered,' Tootie said, before Hannigan could answer. 'Her body's at the dress-shop.'

Hooper scratched his armpit. 'Pity.'

Tootie stepped over to Hooper's desk, jammed her derringer against the man's brow. Beads of sweat sprang out on his forehead but his eyes retained their arrogance.

'I've seen you somewhere before, Marshal.' Tootie's voice came hard. 'I don't know where or when, but I got a feelin' that when I figure it out I am not going to like it one little bit and I'm going to despise you even more than I do already. So you best just keep that fat ass of yours out of my way and give that poor girl a respectable burial.'

Hooper licked his lips. 'I could arrest you for this, Miss.'

'You're welcome to try.' Tootie gave him a cold smile.

Hannigan watched the proceedings with concealed satisfaction, proud of her.

Tootie withdrew the gun from Hooper's forehead, then dropped it into her pocket. The marshal glared but remained where he was, obviously wary of challenging her with the manhunter standing nearby.

Hannigan slid his Peacemaker into its holster. 'I'll be back in the morning to question those men. You best hope nothing happens to them in the meantime.'

Spittle flecked onto the lawdog's beard as he slid his teeth against each other. 'You got no right to come into my town and tell me what to do, Hannigan.'

'Somebody sure as hell has to.' Hannigan backed towards the door. 'You got a job to do, Hooper. 'Bout time you did it.'

Hooper said nothing as they left, but Hannigan felt the lawdog's gaze drilling into their backs.

Once out on the boardwalk he looked at Tootie.

'Reckon you saved my ass again.'

'Getting to be a habit.' She gave him a smile, but little emotion came with it.

'Aurella?'

'Looks like someone strangled her but it was too dark to be sure. Reckon it proves she was into something too big for her.'

He nodded, putting his arm around her as they walked back to the hotel.

'We'll see if those men know anything about it in the morning.'

'You aren't afraid that smelly lawdog won't just let them go?'

He nodded. 'Half-expect him to, but likely they're just hired men anyway and don't know much. Then again, he might be none too eager to test me by releasing them.'

'Unless he's more afraid of someone else.'

'Someone like James Deadwood.'

CHAPTER NINE

With the dawn Jim Hannigan escorted Tootie to the café for a light breakfast. For the most part they ate in silence, Tootie's mind far away, Hannigan's focused on her and the case.

An hour later he left her there and headed to the marshal's office. She'd decided to try talking to Annalea again, assure her there were choices that didn't involve whoring. Hannigan reckoned that was the best thing for her; it would take her mind off her parents' deaths and the men responsible, at least for a short time.

A chill glazed the air, but he reckoned most of the cold came from within him. He saw any chance of a lead drying up like the frost under the morning sun. The two men in the marshal's cell likely harbored little if any information, and Aurella Deadwood had been murdered before he could learn just how deeply she was involved in whatever was going on in this town. Someone had killed her either to keep her quiet or to keep her from reaching an unknown goal.

He wondered what he'd find when he reached

the marshal's office. He expected the worst, that that waste-of-skin excuse for a lawman had let the two bushwhackers go free, but he reckoned it didn't really matter. The chance that they knew anything was remote and Deadwood, or whoever was masquerading as the gunfighter last night, had issued warning that Hannigan and his questions were unwelcome in this town. Likely that attempt would not be the last and efforts would be stepped up to eliminate the threat he posed.

A few moments later he reached the marshal's and his suspicions were confirmed. Upon entering, he paused, gaze sweeping to the cell in which the lawdog had locked his attackers; it was empty. That didn't surprise him but he still had the urge to throttle the sonofabitch.

The thing that made his blood run hot, however, was the sight of the girl, Annalea. She sat in the marshal's chair, knees drawn up to her chest, arms wrapped about her shins. Her green bodice and skirt were soiled with spatters of blood that had obviously come from her swollen bottom lip. A livid bruise marred her right cheek and her left eye had been blackened. Kohl ran from her eyes in dark streaks and her lipstick was smeared. Scratches crisscrossed her bare shoulders. She gazed over at Hannigan, little emotion in her eyes. She appeared stunned, and seemed to be looking right through him.

'What'd he do to you?' Hannigan had trouble keeping his voice level. Anger sent spikes of heat radiating into his cheeks.

She offered him a listless smile. 'Same thing he always does to me. Worse this time, though. He's getting meaner, I think.'

Hannigan could well imagine why: the lawdog, frustrated by his face-offs with Hannigan, perhaps worried about him getting too close to something, had taken it out on the girl. The notion gave him a pang of guilt, though he knew he could not have predicted that the man's reaction would involve the girl.

He sighed, face grim. 'How long you gonna let this go on, Miss? Until he kills you?'

Her demeanor became dark, sad, the look of someone much older, much more tarnished by life than any young woman had call to be. 'Reckon that would be best for me, don't you think? What's the point of goin' on with a life like mine?'

Something in his heart sank. 'How old are you?'

'I'll be sixteen in three weeks.'

Younger than he had thought and the revelation made his stomach cinch. 'Tootie's at the café. Go there. Talk to her, Annalea. Listen to her. Please. There's better than . . . this.'

The girl nodded, uncurled her legs, then stood. 'Was gonna find her anyway. Figured I owed her a favor—'

'Annalea!' the marshal's voice snapped from behind Hannigan. The manhunter whirled, his Peacemaker appearing in his hand almost faster than the eye could follow. The lawdog stopped dead in a doorway that led to a back room.

'Where are they, Marshal?' Hannigan asked,

keeping the gun leveled on Hooper.

The marshal's gaze jumped from him to Annalea, who stood frozen, fear scrawled across her face. 'Get out, you worthless little bitch.'

Annalea looked at the floor. Hannigan swore he had seen a tear start to trickle from her eye. She ran to the door, then out into the morning.

Hannigan's attention jumped back to the marshal. 'I asked you a goddamn question. Don't test your luck lyin' because after seeing what you did to that girl, I confess, there ain't a hell of a lot standing between you and a bullet.'

'Really? You gonna shoot me, manhunter? Kill me for treating a whore poorly?' The marshal tried to put arrogance into his tone, but Hannigan heard fear underlying the bravado.

'Tempted as hell.' Hannigan lowered the weapon and holstered it, but kept his eye on the marshal, who wasn't heeled at the moment. 'Surprised in a town like this that little girl hasn't already done it.'

'I should throw you in jail, you arrogant sonofabitch. Threatening a lawman's a hanging offense in these parts.'

'I don't know what the hell you are, Hooper, but you're no marshal.'

The lawman ignored the remark and went to his desk, widely skirting Hannigan as he did so. He settled into his chair, breath coming hard, eyes cold, hate-filled.

'Had nothin' but your word to hold those men on, Hannigan. Frankly, that ain't worth a damn to me.'

The manhunter approached the desk, leaned over it, both hands gripping the edge. Hooper pulled back slightly. 'Or maybe they knew something you didn't want passed on. Did you send them away, Hooper? Tell them to lie low till I was gone? Or will their bodies turn up burnt beyond recognition at some point?'

Hooper flinched. 'Don't know what the hell you're talking about. You've gone plumb loco.'

'I'm getting damn tired of being run around, you fat sonofabitch. And I know damn well you haven't got the balls to do this yourself. Who's pulling your strings, Hooper? Deadwood? He's alive, ain't he?'

The marshal's eyes narrowed, but a glint of nervousness flickered in them with the mention of Deadwood's name. 'You saw his body.'

'I saw *a* body, one I couldn't identify. But I also saw him in the street last night, didn't I?'

Hooper gave him a smug smile. 'Ghost.'

Hannigan straightened, forcing down his frustration over getting nowhere. 'I don't believe in ghosts, Marshal. But I'm all in favor of putting you in a position where you can find out for yourself if they're real.'

'What the hell's that mean?'

Hannigan went to the door, gripped the handle and looked back to Hooper. 'I've seen your type countless times before . . . lazy, soft, on the take. Take some advice, rethink your part in whatever's going on in this town and come to me with some answers before I come back here with a noose.'

The lawdog's eyes glinted with fury and his face

reddened. 'Let me give *you* some advice, manhunter. You're nothing in this town, and you're nothing to me. Get out before something happens that don't need to.'

Hannigan uttered a chuckle as he opened the door. 'Spoken like a man with someone to back him up, someone with a reputation, maybe . . .' He paused. 'Don't bet your life on reputations, Hooper. They're usually overblown.'

Hannigan stepped out into the morning, leaving the marshal to his thoughts, but knowing men like him rarely saw reason until it was too late.

As the café door opened, Tootie looked up, thinking Hannigan had returned from questioning the men at the marshal's office. Surprise mixed with anger quickened her heart as her gaze settled on the beaten girl who entered. The girl looked about the café, appearing uncomfortable with being in the place after getting a disapproving look from the waitress behind the counter.

'I'll just be a minute,' Annalea said to the waitress. The woman nodded, though from her expression she looked entirely unhappy with having a whore in the café so early in the morning.

Annalea came over to Tootie's table. Tootie beckoned her to sit, then signaled the waitress for a spare cup. After the woman brought it, Tootie poured Annalea a cup of coffee and slid it across the table to her.

'Here, drink this.'

'Thanks,' Annalea said, then gingerly took a sip,

trying to avoid the swollen area of her lip.

Tootie cocked an eyebrow. 'Hooper did this to you?'

Annalea shrugged. 'It's nothin'. He gets rough sometimes but that ain't why I'm here.'

Tootie sighed, frowned. 'He'll kill you one day. The sooner you realize that, the sooner you can make your choice.'

Annalea tried a smile that didn't work. 'Like I told your Mr Hannigan, it would be better that way. I got nothin' to look forward to. No fella would want me now, no decent fella, anyway, and I don't know no other life.'

'My parents were killed when I was six,' Tootie said, a rush of grief cinching a knot in her throat. 'I was sent to live with my aunt, 'cept my aunt didn't want me. She sent me away, to a home. I spent years there, looking forward to nothing but finding the men responsible for taking everything I cared about from me. I'd lost my folks, my brother, and I figured I had nothing but my rage to keep me going. But I was wrong. I just couldn't see what the future held for me. I could have been like you, Annalea. It would have been an easy choice for a girl of sixteen to make when I ran away from that place. But something inside told me there was something better, that someday I would find it, that someday I would find myself.'

The girl shook her head, stared at her coffee. 'Ain't no better out there for me, really, there isn't.'

'You can't know that unless you decide to look for

it. Maybe you're right and there's nothing more for you than what you are now, someone to be used and hurt for another's pleasure.' The girl looked up, her expression that of someone who'd been stung, and Tootie gripped her hand. 'But what if you're wrong? What if you just might be special and there's more waitin' for you than you could ever imagine? That man I'm with, he knows folks. He can provide opportunities if you want them. I can't tell you it will be easy, but, silly as it sounds, if you make the right choices the reward could be a life where you look forward to getting up every morning just because there's a sun in the sky and birds twittering away in a tree.'

'What if I don't know the right choices when they come up?'

'You will. Your heart will tell you. Or more like, you'll know what the wrong ones are and be smart enough to run the other way.'

The girl went silent. Tears shimmered in her eyes. Then her face hardened again. 'That's a fairy tale. It ain't for me.'

Deep sadness swelled within Tootie. For a moment she had thought she'd reached the girl, but she hadn't, and that was that. 'You met me for a reason, Annalea. At least think on what I said.'

Annalea pulled her hand away from Tootie, touching it with her other, her expression growing distant for dragging moments. 'I just came here 'cause I figured I owed you a favor for being nice to me. Most folks don't treat me like I was . . . well like I was anything but a pecker saddle. I saw that man you were lookin' for, last night . . . but he weren't no ghost.'

Surprise flashed across Tootie's face, and her belly dropped. 'Deadwood?'

'Reckon. I was upstairs, had just, well just seen to a fella. It was earlier than I usually work, but this man, he wanted to get his wick dipped 'fore goin' home to his wife, so I brought him up in the afternoon. I was in room three, across the hall from the room where that fella was killed. I seen him sneak into it. I waited a spell, watching through the crack in the door. I saw the marshal come up a bit later and I think I heard them talkin' but couldn't understand what they was saying. The marshal left and I stayed in my room 'cause I was scart. I never saw that fella come back out.'

'You're sure it was him, Deadwood?'

'Reckon as sure as I could be. I saw him the night he rode in. He was in the saloon drinkin' and playin' cards 'fore Tilda took him upstairs.'

Tootie's brow furrowed. 'We searched the room, but it was empty.'

'Reckon he comes and goes somehow, but one thing I'm sure of, he weren't no ghost. Ghost wouldn't use the door, would he? He'd just go plumb through it.'

Tootie nodded, a grim expression crossing her lips. 'There's something about that room, and it has to do with the living, not the dead. I appreciate you telling me.'

The girl smiled a wan smile. 'Don't get yourself killed over it. Please. I'd never forgive myself if

131

anything happened 'cause I told you. I got enough guilt already.'

The girl slid from her chair, then hurried for the door. Tootie watched her go, wishing she could go after her, somehow convince her she had chances if she cared to take them. But it would do no good unless she came to that conclusion on her own.

Her thoughts went to what the girl had told her. Annalea had all but confirmed that Deadwood was alive. Why would he return to the room in which he was supposedly killed?

She aimed to find out. She paid her bill, then left the café. Glancing down the street at the marshal's office, she saw no sign of Hannigan. She reckoned he'd be busy questioning the men for a while yet, so she hurried towards the saloon, one hand in a pocket, fingers wrapped about her derringer. Upon entering the Wild Bull, which served breakfast, she spotted only one customer at the bar. His back to her, he leaned over the counter, barely able to hold up his head. His hat was still on his head; it covered his features. She paid him no more than a glance, since he appeared to be nursing a cup of coffee and likely a hangover.

The barkeep cast her a look that said she had no call being in the saloon but she ignored him and took the three steps down to the saloon proper. With a sideways glance at the fellow, she headed for the stairway.

'Hey, you go no business going up there—' he started.

She whipped the derringer from her pocket and

swung it in his direction. 'Care to argue it with Mr Over-and-Under?'

He raised his hands and shrugged. 'Don't steal anything,' he mumbled, then went back to watering down a bottle of redeye. The man at the bar never bothered to look up. If anything his head lowered.

She hurried up the stairs and along the mezzanine, then scooted down the hall. Stopping in front of room four, she tried the knob, discovering it to be unlocked. She eased the door open, her free hand clamping tighter on the derringer. If Deadwood were in this room. . . .

The thought momentarily froze her. His dark eyes flashed before her memory. For an instant she worried that she might be unable even to pull the trigger if he confronted her, that the sight of him after all these years would cause her to hesitate, lock up, and he would kill her the way he had her mother.

She drew a sharp breath, clenched her teeth. She swung the door all the way inward, then stepped into the room, holding the derringer ready before her. Her gun hand started to shake.

The room was dark, the only light bleeding from a hairline gap running along either side of the drawn shade. She swung the gun right, then left.

'Deadwood!' she said, voice unnaturally loud to cover the fear in it.

No sound came, except the pounding of her own heart.

She moved deeper into the room, eyes adjusting some to the shadows. A crawling sensation moved down her spine. She snapped up the shade and blazing daylight splashed into the room. The glare stung her eyes and she squinted.

The room was empty.

She forced out the breath she had been holding and lowered her gun, then dropped it into her skirt pocket.

She surveyed the room, its sparse furnishings. The bed appeared as if it hadn't been slept in, its sheets and worn blanket pulled tight. A thick coating of dust lay on sections of the floor and near the bed she could see scuff-marks where boots had disturbed it. She noticed other marks from trampling feet, starting at the door and going to the bed, the window and the bureau. Some she could blame on herself and Hannigan, maybe the rest on the whores bringing men up. Studying the marks more closely, she noted that whoever had come in here had gone to the bed, had likely shifted feet nervously.

Deadwood? She doubted he'd be the type to sit around in an empty room shuffling his feet.

She knelt, scrutinized the floor in the sunlight that glazed worn spots and patches of dust. If she recollected right, this room would be above the back part of the saloon, likely a storage area. But she spotted nothing that might have indicated a concealed trapdoor in the boards. On their last case they'd discovered a boy hidden in a compartment under a wagon flooring, but she was certain that wouldn't be the case here.

She stood, hands on her hips, gaze going to the

bed again, then the nightstand, and, at last, the bureau. Her attention focused on the bureau, which also held a thick coating of dust, but she saw nothing unusual about it. She went to it, pulled open the drawers; all three were empty. Her gaze traveled to the floor beside the bureau and for a moment she froze, noting that the dust was disturbed in odd patterns. Some scuffs appeared to be foot traffic but others seemed to vanish right into the wall. She noticed drag marks in an arc, too, as if something had skimmed over the boards.

She reached out, fingers trailing along the wallpaper. She felt a thin line in the papering, peered closer. Nearly impossible to see without being right up on it, she discovered a hairline gap traveling along a vertical stripe in the wallpaper.

'A panel—' she whispered.

Something slammed into the back of her head. She stumbled forward, crashing into the wall face first, then crumpling to the floor. The room whirled before her vision and pain lanced her skull.

A laugh sounded. 'Well, it if isn't the little bitch who damn near kicked my oysters into my throat last night,' came a voice above her. She struggled to focus, saw him then, the man who had been in the barroom when she entered. She hadn't seen his face when he was slumped over his coffee and hadn't given it any thought because she was focused on what Annalea had told her, but now she recognized him as one of the men from the attack last night, the one named Trigg.

The man stepped over her and began pressing points on the wall. With a thin click, then a slight scraping noise, a section of the wall swung out. He jammed his boot beneath her side and rolled her over so he could open the panel all the way. Inside the opening she saw an iron stairway.

'Get up,' Trigg said, motioning with the Smith & Wesson in his hand, likely the thing he had hit her with.

She struggled to her feet, braced herself against the bureau. Her legs shook and her skull throbbed. She'd been lucky he hadn't scrambled her brains.

'Where does it go?' she asked, trying to think of a way to stall him and get to the derringer in her pocket.

'You'll find out soon enough.' He gestured with the gun. 'Get in there and start down. And keep your hands where I can see them.'

She gazed into the opening, then entered, taking the metal stairs slowly, her balance shaky. The steps spiraled down for nearly twenty-five feet, likely right through the downstairs level into a room below the saloon.

When she reached bottom, she stopped, but was prodded forward by the man behind her.

The room was nearly twenty feet square. Another man – the second who'd attacked Hannigan last night – sat in a hardbacked chair, staring at a long table that held piles of strongboxes and canvas bags marked with legends from various banks. Bars of gold and silver lay stacked against the other three walls. Her mouth came open in awe. She reckoned she'd never seen so much money.

Four wall lanterns lit the room, flames turned low. A cot was pushed against the north wall, beside it a table holding a pitcher, whiskey bottles in various states of depletion, piles of cigarette ash and a couple decks of cards.

She froze then, gaze locking on another man who stood in the shadows off to the left.

'Jesus. . . .' she whispered, fear, horror and fury all surging through her at once.

'Not exactly. . . .' said the frock-coated man, stepping into the light.

By the time Jim Hannigan returned to the café Tootie had already left. He hoped she'd been able to talk some sense into Annalea, but he doubted it. Girls who started whoring that young seldom changed for the better. He wondered briefly where Tootie had gone, but reckoned she had left word with the hotel man. He would check after making a stop at the dress shop.

When he entered the shop, he found the owner sweeping the floor, which eliminated any chance of discovering residual clues that might have pointed to the killer. A somber expression was welded to the woman's face. She informed him some men had taken the poor girl's body away, but she reckoned it had been lying there for quite a spell. Since the marshal hadn't bothered doing anything about the body last night the woman had come in this morning to discover Aurella Deadwood's corpse, much to her shock. A foul odor hung in the shop, which

Hannigan didn't care to dwell on. The dress-shop owner then spent the next half-hour complaining about what the news of a murder in her shop would do for business.

Another hour passed without word from Tootie and a nascent worry wormed its way into his mind. Maybe he was just being paranoid because those two men were on the loose, or maybe it was his manhunter's sixth sense kicking in, but he couldn't shake the feeling.

Returning to the hotel only strengthened the notion, because he found their room empty and the hotel manager told him he hadn't seen her since she'd left earlier in the morning. He returned to the café and questioned the waitress, who informed him Tootie had left shortly after a talk with a young woman. The waitress told him that the girl, who she knew worked as a whore, had left first. She also mentioned that the girl kept a room at the boarding-house. Hannigan tried the boarding-house but the girl hadn't been back since early morning, according to the woman who ran the place.

His mind started to concoct various scenarios, none of them encouraging. It wasn't like Tootie just to drop off the face of the earth. She would have left word for him.

Christ, if anything's happened to her. . . .

The thought damn near paralyzed him. He'd come close to losing her on previous cases but things had changed – *he* had changed. He couldn't imagine his life without her now. She'd become part of him. If she were dead. . . .

No, he couldn't let that thought take hold. If he dwelled on that he risked losing all sense of caution and logic. For the moment she was simply missing. Had someone taken her, possibly to use as leverage against him? That was a poor ploy, and whoever was responsible would soon realize that Hannigan would turn this town inside out before backing off the case. They might threaten her life but he knew they would eventually have to kill her anyway when they figured out he would never give up looking for her – or for them.

Could there be another reason she'd been taken? Had she somehow stumbled over something? Deadwood?

Hannigan strode down the boardwalk, out of options and out of patience. Worry was turning into fury. He might not be able to locate Tootie or Deadwood but he could locate two men who he felt certain held some knowledge of whatever was going on in this town. He tried the doctor first, but discovered the man passed out on a couch in his examination room. That likely left him out of the equation and questioning him would produce no results for the time being.

Fifteen minutes later he hurled open the door to the marshal's office. The startled lawman looked up from behind his desk.

'Hannigan, by Christ, ain't I seen enough of you today already?'

The marshal's eyes widened as Hannigan strode around the desk and launched a kick that took

Hooper square in the chest. The marshal flew over backwards, chair and all. He hit the floor with a thunderous bang and rolled sideways, groaning. Hannigan grabbed the toppled chair and hurled it over the desk. A leg shattered as it crashed onto the floor.

The marshal looked up, fear glazing his features. Hannigan kicked him in the jaw. Blood spattered from Hooper's lips and he spat out a tooth.

'Jesus, you loco sonofabitch! What the hell—'

Hannigan doubled, grabbed two handfuls of the fat man's shirt and yanked him close. 'Where the hell is she?'

'Where's who?' The marshal showed genuine surprise and Hannigan's belly sank. He had been damn near certain the man would know something.

'The girl traveling with me. I'm goddamn sure someone's taken her and I got a notion you know who and why.'

'I don't know what the hell you're talkin' about, you crazy sonofa—'

Hannigan banged his forehead into the marshal's nose. Cartilage made a sickening crunch and blood spurted from both nostrils. The nose canted to one side, obviously broken.

The marshal bleated a squeal like a stuck pig, then started to shake and breathe abnormally hard.

'You goddamn better tell me where she is, Hooper. You made a damn fool move taking that girl.'

'I didn't take her! I swear I didn't! I don't know

anything about it, Hannigan. Christ, I ain't that foolish.'

Hannigan studied the man's frightened eyes and despite what he wanted to believe he saw every indication that the man was too scared to lie on that point.

'Where's Deadwood, Hooper?'

'He's . . . he's dead, buried—'

'That ain't the answer I wanted.' Hannigan banged the man's nose a second time and Hooper let out another bleat. Blood spattered onto his beard.

'Please, he's dead, he's dead. . . .'

Now the man *was* lying. His voice had risen to a high-pitched squawk and deeper fear washed into his small eyes.

'I'll tear this goddamn town apart to find her, Hooper. And I'll find Deadwood, too. Best tell him he either gives me back that girl alive or he'll wish to hell he *was* the charred corpse lying in that cemetery.'

The marshal's face darkened and a spark of courage narrowed his eyes. 'You'll never stop lookin' anyway. Why should I make it any easier for you?'

The last measure of restraint deserted Hannigan. He released Hooper's shirt, balled a fist, then pounded it into Hooper's face. The marshal's head rocked like a Hansom with a bad spring. Hannigan hit him again, barely able to stop himself from pummeling the man to within an inch of his life.

He straightened, backed away from the semi-conscious marshal, panting. For one of the few times in his life he was unsure of what to do or where to go next.

CHAPTER TEN

Two hours later Jim Hannigan still hadn't found any trace of Tootie.

As he strode along the boardwalk, the feeling of doom building within him grew nearly overwhelming. Everything about their relationship that he'd feared, working and personal, seemed to be playing out. Someone had struck at him through her, yet so far he'd received no demands, and no one had made contact. Somebody had her and had either killed her by now or was trying to figure out how to use her for leverage. If that somebody were Deadwood, he would know Hannigan's methods and realize that the manhunter would track him to the ends of the earth, no matter what type of ultimatum was issued. Deadwood was smart enough to figure out that Hannigan would never negotiate because either way Tootie's life was forfeit. That made her useless to him. The only window of opportunity for Hannigan was in how long it took the gunfighter to come to that conclusion and realize he had made a mistake, if indeed it was he who had abducted her. That meant if Hannigan had any chance of getting her back alive it would be measured by hours.

You still have no proof it's Deadwood. You don't know for certain he's alive and behind this.

Maybe he did not, but years on the trail had told him to trust his instincts when logic and detective work failed. Right now those instincts assured him the man was alive and involved in her disappearance.

Working on that assumption, where would Deadwood take her? Where could he have grabbed her without being seen?

The room above the saloon?

Was that likely? They had searched the room and if Deadwood were coming and going surely the barkeep would have seen him. Deadwood might have threatened or paid off the 'keep, so Hannigan reckoned a parley with the man was the next order of business. At the same time he could question the girl, Annalea, too, if she were there.

Coming from his thoughts, he stepped off the boardwalk onto the wide main street and headed for the Wild Bull. Footsteps drumming along the opposite boardwalk attracted his attention and he saw Annalea, dressed in a red-sateen bodice and skirt, reaching the saloon a few paces ahead of him.

He motioned to her and as she saw him wave she stopped.

'Miss,' he said and she tensed. He could only imagine the frantic look in his eyes, the worried set of his features, which had likely startled her.

'What's wrong, Mr Hannigan?' she asked, voice

small, as if she were afraid of the answer.

'Tootie's disappeared. I've searched everywhere she might have been. You were the last to see her, at the café. I went looking for you at the boarding-house. . . .'

'I went to the creek to watch the water. I needed to do some thinkin' . . . but I haven't seen her since the café this morning.'

'You have any idea where she might have gone afterward?'

She shook her head. 'No, but I told her I had seen that fella you two are lookin' for.'

'Deadwood?'

She nodded and told him the details of her conversation with Tootie.

'Somethin' about that room. . . .' he mumbled, gazing into the saloon. He thanked the girl, who nodded with a frown, then pushed through the batwings and disappeared into the barroom.

What was it about that room? What made Deadwood go back there, risk being seen? That meant the barkeep was definitely keeping Deadwood's secret and had likely seen Tootie, who Hannigan wagered would have headed straight to the saloon to check out the girl's story.

The manhunter made a move to enter the Wild Bull but before he could do so a drawn-out *skritch* sounded behind him, stopping him cold.

'Turn around slowly, manhunter, and don't even think about going for that gun of yours.'

Hannigan turned, hands raised.

'Marshal. . . .' he said, gaze locking on the

lawman, who stood ten feet diagonally behind him, gun leveled. A moment later another figure stepped off the opposite boardwalk, swaying as he did so. Doctor Butler held a Smith & Wesson, also trained on Hannigan, but shaking in his pale hand.

A third man came from the alley that ran alongside the saloon, fingers clenched on the grip of a Colt. Hannigan recognized him instantly as Beckett, one of the men from the attack the previous night. The hardcase grinned, obviously enjoying the reversal of positions.

Hannigan's lips tightened into a line. He weighed the chances of taking out at least one or two of the men before they killed him but they were spread out and he didn't much care for the odds. With or without Deadwood's direction, Hooper was forcing the situation. And with the confrontation Hannigan knew his time for locating Tootie had run out.

In the room beneath the saloon, Trigg had bound Tootie's wrists and ankles and deposited her in a chair. She watched him as he sat at the table holding the strongboxes, riffling through a deck of cards. He'd been playing solitaire and drinking for the last couple hours.

James Deadwood was alive. The thought shuddered through her mind and ignited burning fury, as well as the childhood terror that had haunted her nightmares for years. Those eyes, those dark dead eyes. Eyes of a man already damned for his crimes. Eyes that reflected only pain and horror and soullessness.

All these years he'd been hiding in plain sight. He didn't recollect her; she felt certain of that. He knew her as nothing more than the partner of a manhunter with whom he had once worked. He'd questioned her, but she'd given him nothing. He was going to kill her; she was certain of that, too. She'd heard him berating Trigg for his stupidity in grabbing her, and that they'd never be able to use her against a man like Hannigan. It was a mere matter of waiting till after the saloon closed late that night to get her body out without being seen.

She eyed the hardcase watching her, disgusted at the looks he'd been casting in her direction over the past few hours. Deadwood had departed a short time ago, leaving her alone with the man after ordering him not to get anywhere near her, or he'd face a bullet. She had no way of getting to the derringer in her skirt pocket and no way of wiggling out of the ropes while he watched her.

She gave the man a smile. If she could get him close enough she might have a chance. But how stupid was he?

The man grinned, licked his lips.

She winked.

'Just how much of an idjit you figure me for?' Trigg asked suddenly. He pulled a knife from his boot and grabbed an apple from the table. He began carving off slices.

'Don't think you're an idiot, just handsome, sugar.' She put as much honey into her tone as possible.

147

'You damn near neutered me last night. Think I want to get close enough to give you a second chance?'

'Thought you weren't scared of an itty bitty girl?'

'You ain't no girl, you're a hellcat.'

'That man Hannigan, he don't pay me all that well. Maybe you could pay me better?'

The man eyed her, as if debating whether she was serious. 'You don't seem like the whore type.'

'I haven't been in the business long.'

His brow cinched. 'All the same, reckon I ain't about to trust you.'

The man wasn't the slickest snake in the woodpile but he had a certain amount of trail smarts and she cursed the fact.

'What's in the boxes?' She nudged her head towards the table. She had to change her tactic if she was to stand a chance of getting out of this alive.

The man shrugged. 'S'pose it don't matter none if you know. Jewels mostly, pieces Deadwood got on his jobs throughout the years.'

'Deadwood your boss?'

The man shook his head. 'No.'

'Who is?'

'None of your goddamn business.'

'I like jewels, sugar. Maybe you could give me one.'

'And have Deadwood blow my brains out? Ain't goddamn likely.'

'He'd never notice one little piece gone.'

The man laughed. 'And just what the hell good

would it do you? You ain't leavin' here on your feet.'

A chill slithered through her innards, but she kept any worry off her face.

'Show me one, then. Least you can do if you're gonna kill me anyway.' She gave him a sugary smile. He studied her, then shrugged.

'Reckon that won't make no difference.'

He set his knife and the remains of the apple on the table, then stood and reached for a strongbox. As he lifted the lid Tootie got a look at an interior overflowing with various pieces of jewelry: neck-laces, brooches, watches, bracelets.

The man's back was partly angled towards her. She had one chance, she figured, and this was it.

She braced herself, knowing it would require perfect timing and balance. With all the strength she could muster she sprang from the chair, her bound ankles holding her feet so close together she had a hard time getting her balance. He was only a few feet away. She hoisted her arms as she half-lunged, half-fell towards him, hoping for the long-shot of getting her bound wrists over his head and around his neck.

The man must've been looking out of the corner of his eye because he spun as she slammed into him. She hit hard, rebounded, unable to get her arms around his neck.

Incapable of staying on her feet, she went over backwards, crashed into the floor half on her side.

Trigg let out a boisterous laugh.

'Haw-haw-haw, you didn't really think that was going to work, did you?' He bent down to grab her to haul her back to the chair.

She smiled. 'No, but I was hoping this might—' Despite throbbing pain in her side, she rolled onto her back, heaved up her bound ankles and slammed her high-laced shoe insteps into his crotch.

A sickening crunch sounded. Trigg's face flashed crimson. 'Oh, goddamn!' he yelled. He doubled, grabbing his middle as blood began streaming from where he'd bitten into his lip.

He collapsed, groaning, squirming. Vomit suddenly gushed from his mouth.

Tootie rolled to the table, kicked up at it until the hardcase's knife fell to the floor. She grabbed the knife and sliced through the ankle ropes, then sawed through the ones binding her wrists.

She threw the knife aside, crawled to Trigg and snatched the groaning man's Smith & Wesson from its holster. After checking the load, she smiled and stood. She glanced at Trigg, deciding he likely wouldn't be any good to his employer for quite a spell and to any woman ever.

Gun in hand, she ran to the metal stairway, then climbed it. At the top the wall panel was closed, but it took her only a moment to find the mechanism that sent it swinging into the room.

By the time she got down the stairs to the barroom proper most of the circulation had returned to her arms and legs. She saw Annalea poised at the batwings, peering out at something in the street. The barkeep cast her a threatening look, but made no move towards her.

'What's happening?' Tootie asked, as she reached Annalea.

The bargirl's face welded with shock, but it came mixed with a huge measure of relief. 'Your friend, Mr Hannigan. Marshal and the gunfighter fella's got him cornered. The doc and another man's with him. I think they're gonna kill him.'

Tootie's blood raced. She pushed the young woman aside and plunged through the batwings out into the waning afternoon.

'What the hell is this, Marshal?' Jim Hannigan asked as he stepped into the middle of the street.

'No further, Mr Hannigan. 'Less you want me to shoot you right where you stand.'

'You'd risk killing me in broad daylight?'

'No one in this town would give a damn, I reckon.'

Hannigan's gaze locked with the lawdog's. 'A lot more sure of yourself with these men backing you up, aren't you, Hooper? What the hell's going on in this town anyway? Who the hell are you?'

The lawdog laughed, but Hannigan noticed Butler shaking harder, his aim wavering. Butler was the weakest link, likely the worst shot. That meant he had to take out the lawman and the other first.

'Name's Edgecomb. I was Deadwood's partner.'

'So he's alive?'

'He's alive. We ain't rode together in quite a spell, but I been his vault-tender for years – for a sizable cut, of course.'

'Care to tell me the details, since I reckon you're

going to kill me anyway?'

Hannigan's hand lowered a fraction, but the lawdog gestured with his gun, making him raise it again.

'This the part where you stall, Mr Hannigan? Get me to tell my story while you figure a way out of your predicament?' The lawdog laughed again, a mocking sound. 'There's no way out. Not after what you did to me this morning. And no way out for your gal, neither.'

'Where is she?' The question came through gritted teeth.

'She's alive – for the moment. Deadwood's got her.'

'This was a damn fool move, Edgecomb,' came a voice from the batwings. A man stepped out of the saloon and crossed the boardwalk, his frock-coat jostled by the breeze, his dark eyes glittering beneath his battered hat. 'Mr Hannigan could likely shoot at least two of you 'fore you even blinked, and I'm guessin' it's obvious which two it'd be.'

James Deadwood stopped in the middle of the street, roughly ten feet from Jim Hannigan. The man still made an imposing figure. Gunfighter, legend, cold-blooded killer. Deadwood was all of those and certainly no ghost.

The marshal frowned. 'No more fool than grabbing that girl and getting Hannigan all riled up over it.'

Deadwood chuckled without humor. 'I might remind you, Edgecomb, it was your man who was stupid enough to be sitting in the saloon when she walked in, though I reckon he had damn little choice but to grab her after she went looking around in that room.'

'How is it you're alive, Deadwood?' Hannigan asked. 'Whose body's in that grave outside of town?'

Deadwood smiled. 'Who knows? Some passer through? Edgecomb?' Deadwood glanced at his partner; the lawdog shrugged. 'My former partner, Mr Edgecomb, here, runs a nice little operation. For a price he can make any owlhoot appear dead.'

Hannigan nodded. 'And you wanted to appear that way because you were close to a hangman's noose. . . .'

Deadwood's eyes narrowed. His voice lowered, grew dark. 'Reckon it was time to start a new life, enjoy my gains. Couldn't do that with the law on my ass.'

'So you had Edgecomb and his friends arrange your death. Why you still in town?'

'Takes time for the transport coach to get here from Mexico. I got a lot to haul with me. If you'd have just stayed out of it I would have been gone in another week. Gotta admit, though, was fun readin' all the nice things the papers writ about me and seein' a legendary manhunter whirlin' around like a dog lookin' for snakes.'

'Your daughter?'

He laughed. 'Aurella wasn't my daughter. She was just some whore who figured she could cut herself a piece of the pie. Reckon I got a bad habit of running at the mouth when I'm drunk.'

Hannigan studied the man, noting the Colts

shoved into his waist sash. He might take out Edgecomb and Beckett, but Deadwood was too big a factor even by himself. How fast was he? Hannigan didn't know but if his reputation was even half right. . . .

Deadwood must have picked up on the thought because he grinned. 'You can't do it, Hannigan. You never could have beaten me alone. With these men here you'd be dead 'fore your gun even cleared leather.'

'Would he?' came Tootie's voice as she burst through the saloon doors. She kept the Smith & Wesson in her hand aimed high, trained on Deadwood.

Deadwood didn't even glance at her. 'I see Edgecomb's idiot hardcase did his job 'bout the way I expected.'

'You killed my mother, you sonofabitch!' She came forward a step, fingers white as she squeezed the gun. Edgecomb and the hardcase didn't waver their aim from Hannigan, obviously considering him the more dangerous threat.

Deadwood's brow cinched. 'Don't know what you're talkin' about, ma'am.'

Tootie's face darkened. 'New Mexico, thirteen years back. You were on the run. You took my mother into the kitchen and figured on doing things to her but you never got the chance after your partner killed my father.'

Deadwood shrugged. 'Forgive my poor recollection, but I killed so many it don't matter to me to keep one worthless woman in mind.'

Edgecomb suddenly burst out laughing. 'I recollect it. Your pa bleated like a baby lamb when I put a bullet in him!'

Hannigan saw it coming, and at the last second maybe Edgecomb did too, because his gun jerked up just a fraction before Tootie's Smith & Wesson swung around and blasted a shot. Edgecomb jolted, then looked down at his chest, at the scarlet orchid blossoming just beneath his tin star. His gun dropped from his nerveless fingers.

'Oh, hell. . . .' the lawdog muttered, then pitched forward face first into the dirt.

Deadwood smiled unsympathetically. 'He had that comin', I reckon. Never did know when to keep his mouth shut.'

As Deadwood finished speaking Beckett suddenly swung his gun towards Tootie. She saw it and tried to adjust her own aim, throwing herself sideways at the same time.

That sideways lunge saved her from taking a bullet in the chest. Lead singed across her shoulder and reflexively she jerked the trigger of her Smith & Wesson. The gun went off, bullet punching into the boardwalk. The recoil kicked the weapon from her grip and it spun to a stop on the boardwalk ten feet away. Tootie slammed into the saloon wall, then slumped to the ground, clutching her shoulder. Blood trickled between her fingers.

The hardcase lowered his aim for a second shot, a malicious expression riding his features.

Hannigan started to twist, his hand moving down despite Butler's gun being still leveled on him.

'Don't, Mr Hannigan!' shouted Butler, straight-arming his gun with both hands, but Hannigan ignored him.

Before Hannigan's hand reached his Peacemaker a shot rang out. A panicked thought told him he was too late, the hardcase had fired, killed her.

But Beckett froze, the vicious expression vanishing from his face. His gun fell to the boardwalk. His mouth came open; blood streamed from the corner and ran down his chin. He fell forward, slammed into the ground and lay still.

Standing just outside the batwings was the bargirl, Annalea, a rifle she had likely grabbed from the barkeep jammed to her shoulder. She lowered the rifle, then went to Tootie, who was half-way to her feet, and helped her up.

A surge of relief cascaded through Hannigan but he had not even a second to dwell on it. He swung on instinct, his hand sweeping the rest of the way to his gun in the same motion. His Peacemaker came up, jerked left, and he triggered a shot.

Doc Butler jumped backwards, a bullet punching into his chest. The sawbones hit the ground hard, his gun flying off into the dirt.

Hannigan's aim swept back to Deadwood without hesitation. Deadwood smiled a frozen smile and held his palms up.

The manhunter eyed the man. Here was the butcher who had murdered Tootie's mother, likely scores of other innocent folk.

His expression hardened and he slid his Peacemaker back into its holster.

Tootie was on her feet and had taken the rifle from Annalea, who stood at her side. She aimed it at Deadwood, arms shaking.

'You going to let your partner just shoot me?' Deadwood asked Hannigan, arrogance in his tone. 'That ain't the manhunter's code, now, is it, Hannigan?'

Tootie uttered a chopped sound of disgust. 'I'm not going to shoot you, you bastard, but I'll see you hang and enjoy every minute of it.'

'He won't hang.' Hannigan's hazel eyes locked with Deadwood's, a grim finality sweeping across them. 'He's too dangerous to face a trial where his legend might overcome his guilt in the eyes of a jury. Go for your gun, Deadwood. Your reputation says you're the fastest draw who ever lived. Let's find out if that's true.'

Deadwood stared into Hannigan's eyes, didn't move. 'I won't draw on you, Hannigan. You'll have to bring me in. Everyone in this country deserves a fair trial.'

The gunslinger's tone confirmed everything Hannigan had just said. The man knew he stood a better chance of getting off legally than of winning a contest against someone who might prove his equal.

'Like I said, I won't take that chance with you, Deadwood. Draw or I'll kill you where you stand.' Hannigan's hand hovered over his Peacemaker. For the first time he caught a flicker of fear in Deadwood's gaze.

'You won't shoot me, Hannigan. You hero types

don't gun down men in cold blood.' Deadwood's tone came without the arrogance now. He wasn't certain of his own words.

Hannigan's expression didn't change. 'I'm no hero.'

Before Hannigan even finished the words Deadwood went for his gun. The gunslinger had realized he had no choice and had tried to seize the advantage.

Hannigan was prepared for him. His hand swept for his Peacemaker.

The gunslinger's reputation was no lie. Deadwood was the fastest draw Hannigan had ever encountered. His hand motion was blurred and the Colt appeared in his grip as if it had materialized there.

Both men's shots blended into one terrific roar.

Deadwood's lips pulled into a strained smile.

Hannigan froze.

'What they say about accuracy and speed . . . bein' a myth . . .' Deadwood said, voice shaky. 'Reckon they was wrong after all. . . .'

The gunslinger dropped his Colt and crumpled to his knees. His fingers went to the splotch of crimson above his heart. He uttered a liquidy sound, then fell forward, unmoving.

Hannigan slid the Peacemaker back into its holster. He clutched the bloody spot on his biceps where Deadwood's bullet had gored a superficial wound.

Tootie dropped the rifle and came running over to him, throwing her arms around his waist.

'Never seen anything so fast. . . .' Hannigan mumbled, gaze riveted on the dead gunslinger.

Tootie smiled. 'That's only 'cause you can't see yourself.'

With the dawn three days later, Jim Hannigan and Tootie del Pelado saddled their mounts and led them out of the livery. Hannigan had made arrangements to have Deadwood's body shipped back to his Pinkerton friend for confirmation, as well as Edgecomb's. Trigg, the remaining hardcase, sat in the marshal's jail, guarded by a county deputy for whom Hannigan had telegraphed.

After mounting, they set their horses into a slow walk. He was only too happy to see this town behind them. Tootie had said little since Deadwood's death, and he knew she was thinking about her parents, coming to terms with the fact that the mystery of who had murdered them had been solved and that part of her past could now be closed. Grief would go on, perhaps always, but he knew she felt better knowing who had killed them, and knowing those men had paid for their crime.

A girl came running out into the street from the boarding-house a block down, pulling him from his thoughts. Annalea had dressed in a blue-flowered gingham dress and had a small canvas bag tucked beneath her arm. She'd scrubbed the kohl and coral from her face and now looked her fifteen years of age.

As they reined up she peered up at him, then at Tootie. 'I bought me a new dress at the shop.'

Tootie gave her a soft smile, held out a hand. The girl came up to her, passed her the bag, which Tootie secured to the saddle.

'See, you knew the right choice after all. . . .' Tootie slid forward a bit, offering her hand to the girl.

Annalea smiled and grabbed Tootie's hand. She jammed a foot into the stirrup and with Tootie's help swung into the saddle behind her.

'Reckon it's the first of many,' said Annalea, smiling, as Tootie gigged the horse into an easy walk.

Hannigan followed suit, thinking for the first time in a long time that their mission just maybe did make a bit of a difference in this blood-drenched world they called the West.